Half on Tuesdays

Enjoy!
Amy E. Whitman

Amy E. Whitman

Brandylane
Publishers, Inc.
Publishing books since 1985

ISBN: 978-1-947860-71-1

LCCN: 2019909646

Designed by Michael Hardison
Production management by Christina Kann

Printed in the United States of America

Published by
Brandylane Publishers, Inc.
5 S. 1st Street
Richmond, Virginia 23219

brandylanepublishers.com

*Dedicated to the enduring friendship
of Sandy and Marie.
And to all of those whose lives are
affected by the "Evil Agent A."*

—A.E. Whitman

April 3

Dear It,

This feels really weird. I mean, here I am: 13 years old, old enough to be in junior high, and I'm writing in a "diary." Like, how babyish. My mom, who is all about "reading" and "writing," got it in her head that a very special 13th birthday present for me would be this dumb journal. No offense, but I'm about music and friends and getting my ears double-pierced. I'm not about writing in a journal, which makes a perfect gift for a NERD! I'm not a nerd. So why does Mom think I'd write stuff down in a stupid notebook journal? Or whatever you call it.

Happy Sweet 13!!!!! Nothing about this journal makes it sweet. In all fairness, though, I did get some cool clothes and a two-piece to die for. Can't wait till I can wear it! Well, bye, I guess.

Signed,
Whatever

May 7
Dear It,

I know what you're thinking. Why am I writing again in this dumb journal? For starters, my phone's been taken away because I was caught texting past my curfew time of 10:00. So no phone for the next three hundred years! Okay, more like three days. How am I supposed to function in my day-to-day life? I even told Mom I needed it for some of my classes because we do research on our phones. She didn't budge. So I guess I'm writing because I had a bad day at school and because I can't use my phone. I needed to rant to someone. Jason and I broke up, again, and I think this time it's for good. I feel like never being a person ever again. Like, I want to turn invisible or something.

I talked to my mom about it. She helped some. I don't know. I guess it's hard for her to get it because she and my dad divorced two years ago. So the whole opposite-sex-relationship stuff isn't high on her priority list. Her advice was that people fade in and out of relationships, and you just have to make the best of it. Even if that means moving on. So, here I am without my boyfriend to go to the May formal. I guess I'll go with the girls.

Oh my gosh—what if I see him there? Then what? Like, what do I do? Just stand there in my deep purple satin dress staring at his matching purple tie? Just standing there all awkward with each other? What if he asked another girl, and she's with him? You're right: I'll be staring at her. I'll stare her down so much that she'll run to the bathroom and stay there (if she knows what's good for her).

Then, while she's in the bathroom, I'll accidentally-on-purpose grind my high heel into Jason's "prized" soccer foot! Why does life have to be so confusing? He was always about his soccer, and I was his afterthought. My mom said that writing things out on paper can help clear your mind and release your feelings. Clear my MIND!! Release my FEELINGS!! At this moment, I want to explode! Explosions of tears, anger, jealousy, hurt, and pride all freaking at once. BOOM!!!!! Huge explosion of emotional guts all over this page!

My eyes turn blue when I cry. Yeah, kind of freaky. As I cry, my eyes go from green to blue. I don't know why I'm telling you this. I guess I thought it could be something about me I could tell you. So now you know.

Signed,

Your loss, Jason

June 3

Dear It,

Since I told you all about the break-up and the May formal without Jason, I thought I would follow up with the actual drama that took place. I did go to the formal with a group of girls. We weren't exactly the rejects, but we came close. Jason was there with some guy friends, but I stayed out of his way. I know I was all about heeling him in the foot before, but my friends said that he wasn't worth it, and I would just start a war. So I stayed clear of him as much as I could. The music was great, but I wasn't much into it. I did look pretty sweet in my dress. It was weird getting pics without Jason standing next to me. He still wore his suit with the matching purple tie. I wanted to think he looked ugly, but man, did he look hot!!!

Well, I did get some eye contact with him. He was hanging out with his friend Ken just inside the entrance door. I had to pass by them to meet up with Emily. (She was a mess the whole night. She broke up with her boyfriend, Zac, just two weeks before, and she couldn't keep it together. Every time she saw him, she would tear up and run for the bathroom.) Well, I was going to the bathroom to check on her, and I was so shook!—there stood Jason. So, our eyes met for a sec or two. In all honesty, he looked a bit sad. Yeah, that was enough for me to chill. I don't know. See what happens. Good sign, though. He didn't come with another girl.

Signed,
Relieved but lonely

June 17

Dear Journal,

I'm writing again—what the heck. I feel like you should be addressed a little kinder. I mean, I would hate it if someone called me "It" all the time. So, since this notebook is supposed to be a journal, I can at least call you "journal." But don't get any ideas about how I'm going to name you like some pet pony. Remember, I'm 13, and being 13 makes me officially a teenager. Not a tween or a preteen, an official teenager. And to top it off, my parents are "suggesting" that I get a volunteer-type job to do over the summer. Excuse me; I'm doing whatever. If a job comes my way, yeah, I'll work some. But this is my summer time off!

Speaking of my parents. My dad's birthday was on Father's Day this year. So I spent the weekend at his place. No shocker here, but my older brother was there too. You see, my brother lives with my dad for the most part, while I live with my mom. It stinks, I know, but I'm okay with it. At first, it was both of us living with Mom, and off on the weekends to Dad's. But now, we have me living with Mom and my brother, Forrest, living with Dad.

I might as well tell you some about my dad. He is six-foot-even. He has sandy red hair with a light complexion. My mom calls him the "hippie gone metro." He used to be a free spirit like my mom. You know, get in the VW and drive to wherever until the gas runs out. No map, no plans; just go. But over the years, his environmental engineering job went full-blown career. Well, let's just say the VW trips got less and less frequent, while the job demands got more and more intense.

My dad turned 56 on June tenth. I know this is going to sound creepy and all, but if I look at him closely, I can see around the edges a pretty good-looking guy. He does take care of himself. He is all about protein shakes and organic veggies. He isn't extreme or anything. But I can see why my mom would dig the looks of my dad. He has the smarts to be just about anything he would want to be. So he chose engineering. He went into environmental stuff because he wanted to save the earth. Now, he just wants to save his bank account from going below five digits.

Oh, I guess I didn't mention his name. Todd Whitcomb the Third. Sounds stuffy, doesn't it? Well, that's what my mom thought the first few times they met. Of all places, they met at a rally in protest of killing muskrats. That's a whole other story for another time. I've written way too much already. Writing isn't that bad. But don't count on me getting used to it.

Signed,

My name is Summer Ray Whitcomb

P.S. *Since you know what my name is, I guess I should tell you some about what I look like. I'm five feet two inches tall (short, if you ask me). I have strawberry blonde hair with green eyes. I have faded freckles lined up across my cheek bones. My nose is too chubby for my face. My shoulders are a bit too broad for my slender torso. I'm good with how I look. But my feet could be bigger. It's hard to find shoes my size without being in the kiddie section.*

July 5
Dear Journal,

Oh my gosh! I'm so shook. I saw Jason at the park! Every year, we go to Sunset Park to see the fireworks for the Fourth of July. It's one of the few times throughout the year that we go as a family. This means Mom, Dad, me, and Forrest. Well, I walked down the hill to the concession stand to get in line, and standing right in front of me was Jason! I froze. I didn't know what to do. So I cleared my throat like they do in the movies. I made that noise that sounds like a bad intercom connection to hopefully get his attention. Well, in the movies they do it once, and the person catches on. I had to make the noise three times until Jason turned around.

Get this: he turns around and says, "I knew you were behind me. I watched you coming down the hill."

I said, "Oh, well, I knew it was you because I watched you stand in front of me." HOW STUPID OF A THING TO SAY!!!!!

But he gave me a boyish smile, which made me smile. And then, like a gentleman, he let me order before him. But when I turned around after placing my order to tell him thank you, he was gone. We spoke to each other, and in my utter stupidity I made him smile!

Signed,
Summer the Hopeful

July 22

Dear Journal,

My mom's birthday is coming up. I need some advice as to what to get her. It was easy for my dad. I just get him a gift card to Starbucks, and he's happy. He practically lives there when he isn't at work. He loves his coffee. Mom is different. How would I describe my mom? For starters, she has the most geekish job in the world. She's the head librarian at the Montville Public Library. She is constantly telling me how she goes to a thousand different places in one day as she connects readers with books. I don't get it, but she loves her job. She describes herself as "an advocate of all living things, a friend to the friendless, and a lover of words." She has knighted herself as being Gary Paulsen's most loyal reader. (Her version of Heaven would be forever eating breakfast with the man.) She also considers herself an experienced free spirit. She believes that life's fulfillments can only be found within the corners of life's adventures.

My mom means a lot to me. She gets on my nerves, like yeah, that's normal. But she really tries to be the best mom she can be. I guess it's the little things that stick with me the most. Like, when I'm sick, she still pampers me. Or when she comes home from work, she has my favorite candy bar hanging out of her coat pocket. Really, I love how she tells me that she thinks of me throughout her day. I know that I'm important to her. I just want to find the perfect gift for her this year.

Signed,
Summer the hopeless gift-finder

August 1
Dear Journal,

Mission accomplished! My mom, who by the way is named April, totally loved my gift! Well, it was more of a new gift on top of an old idea. While I was growing up, my mom would keep a scrapbook of my childhood memories. Stuff like my baptism certificate, a clump of hair from my first haircut, a piece of cloth that I had to have while I sucked my thumb, pictures and cards from relatives no longer living. I love this scrapbook. I still look at it now and again. Well, she stopped putting stuff into it around the time of the divorce. It's all good with me, but I hope someday if I have kids, I can do the same for them.

Anyhow, this gave me the idea for my mom's gift. I picked out a really nice card and wrote in it that from this point on, I'm going to put together a kind of scrapbook for her. Our memories are going to come from our Tuesday Times. Every Tuesday, she and I are going to hang out for a couple hours. We might go out to eat, we might see a movie, or we might go bowling or just walk around town. At the end of our time together, I'm going to save a piece of something to put in the scrapbook I'm making her. The scrapbook is perfect. It has a floral design with a peacock that reminds you of a fancy garden. As the book fills up, so will the memories of our Tuesday Times together.

My mom cried the biggest happy tears I have ever seen her cry. She's weird that way. She cries when she's really happy or when something really means a lot to her.

Our first Tuesday Time is in four days. She's going to choose what we're going to do. It's only fair that she gets to pick the first one since it's for her birthday. She has hinted to me that we aren't going anywhere. Hope I can do this. If it's staying home all the time, I think I'll go insane.

Oh, by the way, my mom turned the speed limit. 55 years old!!!!!!

Signed,
Summer the awesome gift-giver

August 4

Dear Journal,

I wasn't looking forward to Tuesday Time with Mom. At first I thought, "That's trash," and wanted to reschedule. I was at the pool most of today. The drama got so thick that I just left. Emily and Zac, who had broken up, got back together again just to be miserable. I mean, Emily is the jealous type. She got all mad because she thought Zac was looking at other girls. If you don't trust your boyfriend, then don't go to the pool together. Because then Zac said that for all he knew, Emily was checking out guys to get back at him. Zac isn't the buff dude type, so he got all spastic about it. He kept telling Emily that he wasn't looking at other girls. He told her over and over that he just wanted to swim with her.

Jason and I are who-knows-where in our break up. Nothing awful is going on, like he isn't dating someone else. But then, he isn't saying much to me either. I see him around, but not a lot because he's always at soccer practice. And if he isn't at soccer practice, then he's at soccer camp. And if he isn't at soccer camp, he's playing in a tournament. Oh, I just got so mad at Emily and Zac that I left the pool. When I got home, I remembered it was Tuesday. Mom wasn't home yet from work. I can't ditch her on the very first one. Write to you later.

Signed,
Summer the drama sick

August 6

Dear Journal,

I couldn't fall asleep, so I thought I'd write to you. Of all the things my mom wanted to do for our first official "Tuesday Time," it was baking. At first I had some attitude because, on top of the pool drama, I got sunburn on my shoulders. But after a while, I started getting into it. We made—or should I say we baked a homemade apple pie. Like, not from stuff already made. We made it all from scratch. We made the crust. We peeled the apples, melted the butter, added the sugar, sifted the flour, cracked the eggs, and listened to mom's favorite music. We danced our way all around the kitchen. We pigged out on ice cream, eating it right out of the carton. Then had some more ice cream a la mode with our warm tasty pie! Mom told me that, when I was little, she used to sing this song to me while she rocked me to sleep. It goes like this:

I love you, I love you,

I love you, I do.

I think you're a peachy pie

And the apple of my eye.

For my very first memory maker, I'm going to write down the words of this song. I'm not crafty, but I'll try making an apple out of red paper, then glue the words of the song on it with a picture of us taking a bite out of our homemade pie. This Tuesday Time together just might work out after all.

Good night,

Summer the apple pie baker

August 8

Dear Journal,

My mom and I got into an argument. Sometimes she gets in my face and just lets me have it. Well, this time it was for my own good. I was all depressed like, you know, in one of my moods, and she tried to talk to me about it—but I don't give her any credit. Finally, she said to get over myself, go to one of Jason's games, and take it from there. You know, just see what happens. Well, I just lay there on the couch acting like I couldn't care less. Then she really got royal with me. "Summer Ray, that couch isn't your throne, and you aren't the queen of this house." Yeah, she was right, but I wasn't going to let her know that. So I got up and went to my room. Sometimes I feel so heavy inside. So heavy that it's hard to even walk.

Signed,
Summer the Slug

August 9

Dear Journal,

Today I think is the day I can get deep with my writing. Baring a part of my soul is going to hurt. Today is an anniversary of the day my best friend, Mettisha Marie Calhoun, died in a tragic car accident. It was three years ago, and she was only 10 years old. We were supposed to become teenagers together. But she never will.

We were beyond being friends—we were sisters. We did everything together. We went to birthday parties, roller skating, bike riding, and sledding together. We dreamed of being in each other's weddings after, of course, going to prom and being roommates in college. We were supposed to grow up together. And now we never will.

It's hard to write. I'm crying too hard. I just want to stop writing. I'm sliding down that steep slope of sadness again. I don't want to feel the pain. I can't stop writing. No, I won't stop writing. In memory of her, I have to keep on writing.

Everyone called her "Metti" for short. Exactly three years ago today, Metti and her mom were driving home from the mall. They had been back-to-school shopping. They were on the highway, crossing over a bridge, when a pickup truck smashed into their car head-on. The pickup truck went swerving to the right, hitting another car, while Metti and her mom's car went spinning into the concrete wall of the bridge. Metti was sitting up front in the passenger's seat, and that was the side of the car that got hit the hardest. The airbags went off, and they were wearing their seatbelts, but it wasn't enough to save Metti's life.

The impact of the crash hitting the wall broke every bone in her body. It is hard for me to keep writing, but I'm writing for Metti. She pretty much died at the scene. So she didn't suffer. I know she's in God's care. I know I'll see her someday. Metti's mom, Janet, survived. She has to walk with a cane because of nerve damage in her right leg. Metti's dad and two brothers were home at the time of the accident. So they are alive and well.

I'm not well. I miss you, Metti. I miss you so much. I got to thinking. It's been a while now, and I keep writing to you. I was sort of rude in the beginning, thinking that keeping a journal was childish. I don't think that so much anymore. Did you know there are famous people in history who kept journals? Lots of them were even adults. Some of them were explorers, runaway slaves, Civil Rights marchers, or prisoners of war.

One of the most famous diary authors was a 13-year-old Jewish girl named Anne Frank. Her diary has been translated into dozens of languages and made into plays and even a movie. So, I look at it as being part of a club without the other members knowing about it.

To be fair to you, journal, and to feel as though my best friend is still with me, I am naming you Metti. My dear Metti. Naming you this will make it more personal when I write to you. Anne Frank named her diary "Kitty," so I think it's okay to name you, too. Metti you shall be. I know you can't talk back and say if you like this idea or not. I know there will be times when I feel alone. So writing to you will be like writing to my friend.

Signed,
Summer, who will always remember you and will always be your best friend

Rest in peace,
Mettisha Marie Calhoun.
Rest in peace.

August 11

Dear Metti,

It seemed a bit crazy writing your name. But I like it. Today was our second Tuesday Time, and Mom got to pick again. She came home from work and said, "Thank goodness today is Tuesday, because for our Tuesday Time we're going out for dinner. I'm way too tired to cook. Summer, you good with that?" I told her it was a no-brainer. I even offered to drive since she was so tired. (I didn't stand a chance on that one.) We're off to Marco's Pizza Palace. We'll share a pizza with side salads, and if I can, I'll try to get ice cream for dessert!

Signed,
Summer,
who wants pizza, salad, and ICE CREAM!

August 12

Dear Metti,

I'm still stuffed from all the pizza Mom and I ate! And yes, I got my ice cream. For my memory keeper, I kept a napkin from Marco's Pizza Palace. All through our meal, we spoke like royalty. We tried adding a British accent to everything we said. I laughed so hard at Mom's accent that my soda came out my nose! A good time, but quite embarrassing.

Signed,
Summer the Soda Snorter

August 14

Dear Metti,

I haven't written to you at all about the times I go to my dad's. So, I thought I'd do that in this entry. It's about 10:00 at night. Forrest is still up talking on the phone to his friend Chip. It's his nickname for Charles. Chip is a good guy. He's lots more fun than Forrest. Forrest isn't fun. He doesn't just play to play. He has to have a purpose to everything in life. Chip plays around, you know—goes to the courts and hangs out playing basketball with whoever shows up and wants to play. He's like everybody's big brother. He has your back. If the players get too rough, he calms them down. Even those who pick fights respect him. I wish Forrest would be more like Chip. Forrest has to have an ultimate goal to whatever he does. If a goal can't be formulated and/or achieved, then to Forrest it's all a waste of time. One word for that—BORING!

Anyway, we had Chinese for dinner, then we watched a movie that was all about agents, bombs, and blackmail. I got bored, so I fell asleep. Now I'm wide awake in my dad's spare bedroom, writing to you. This room isn't like my room at home, but it is what it is. (What the heck—I sound just like my dad!)

Here's more about my brother. He is 20 years old. He has my mom's rich cedar-red hair and perfect nose. I mean perfect. Their noses are just the right thickness and length. I call them "statue" noses. Forrest has bold brown eyes like my mom and rounded edges to his shoulders and hips. (Well, because he's a guy, he doesn't have to worry about his hips.) He has always been into nerdy stuff like playing Battleship, making science fair projects, and don't forget making money. He started making money at nine years old. After stormy days, he would walk around the neighborhood offering to pick up sticks in people's yards and bundle them up. He would come home with a stack of dollars! Yeah, okay, he earned it. But what about having a childhood?

Because he's seven years older than me, we've never had much to do with each other. He decided to go live with Dad after enrolling at Mercer Community College. Dad says, "In the name of saving money," which is a way of making money, it's cheaper to get his core classes over with at a community college, then transfer to a four-year college. Forrest has brains like I have hairs on my legs. He can be whatever he wants to be. He'll do it, just like Dad.

Wow, I never thought I'd write this much about my brother. Gotta sleep now. I won't be surprised if I have dreams about agents, bombs, and blackmail.

Signed,
Summer the Double Agent

August 15

Dear Metti,

   Still at my dad's apartment. Not much happening. Catch you up when I get home.

Signed,
Summer is bored

August 16

Dear Metti,

Finally, I'm home! Mom said that nothing happened while I was gone. To be honest, something is happening. When I opened the refrigerator, I discovered Mom had put a dirty cereal bowl next to the milk. She said it belonged there. I wasn't sure if she was serious or pranking me. My mom is such a weirdo.

Mom did mention, though, that she knows what we're going to do for this week's Tuesday Time. Part of me is excited, and part of me is nervous. What if she takes me to bingo night at the local firehouse? She randomly talks about doing that. You know, having someone to go with and share in her winnings. Oh, I sure hope not.

Signed,
Summer, who won't have to wash dishes because dirty dishes belong in the refrigerator.

August 17

Dear Metti,

I just couldn't wait to tell you. I Facetimed with Emily, and after she told me all about her Zac issues, she finally got to what she really wanted to tell me. I could just scream... Okay, I screamed! She told me that she heard from Zac, who heard from his cousin's friend, who is on the same soccer travel team as Jason, that Jason still likes me! I'm so jumpy right now!

When I want to, I can put something out of my mind and just not think about it. My mom says I'm strong like that. So, ever since my mom got in my face about going to one of Jason's soccer games—well, I just put him out of my mind. It wasn't that I didn't want to support him by seeing him play. It's just that I couldn't imagine myself being at his game when soccer is the main thing that got between us. So I got stubborn and mentally said no to most everything about Jason.

BUT NOW THAT HAS ALL CHANGED!!!!!!! HE STILL LIKES ME!!!!! Emily said that Jason said to Zac's cousin's friend while they were on the bus that he misses having a girlfriend to do stuff with, like movies and roller skating and stuff like that. So Zac's cousin's friend asked him who he would have as a girlfriend. Jason said that he still would want me because I can make him laugh about silly stuff. He said it helped him not be so serious with his soccer all the time. I kind of gave him mental breaks. HE STILL LIKES ME!!!!!

Got to text Racheal and Liz and the whole rest of the world!

Signed,

Summer, the girl Jason still likes!!!

24

August 18
Dear Metti,

I'm so nervous. Today is Tuesday, and Mom went to work all smiles about our Tuesday Time. I faked a smile back at her. I can't fake being sick. It just wouldn't be right. Gotta go for a long walk to work out my nerves. Write to you later.

Signed,
Summer, who is
so NERVOUS! ("G4" BINGO)

August 18 (later)

Dear Metti,

You really have to hand it to my mom. SHE TOOK ME TO JASON'S SOCCER GAME!!!!!!!!!!!!!!!!!!!!!!!!!!!!!!!!

She was all worried that I would be embarrassed because I was there with a parent. But when we drove into the grassy parking lot, I almost DIED! There across the field, Jason's soccer team was warming up. I saw him from a distance, so that made me just not move. I mean, I sat in the front seat, just staring straight ahead. My mom nudged me on my shoulder and said she was getting out. Then she got out. She pulled two chairs from the trunk and walked away, leaving me in the car.

I took some deep breaths and thought about how my insides felt like a sword was sticking through me. I know he still likes me now, so I was all worked up. But he doesn't know that I know that he still likes me, so that made me more worked up.

Then I saw my mom sitting in her chair with an empty chair next to her. For some reason, it made me laugh. Like, there sat my mom with her imaginary friend. So I got out of the car. In my head, I yelled at my legs to walk to the chair. I sat down, and Mom said, "Summer, dear, you're sitting on my imaginary friend." It scares me how much we can be alike.

Jason's team won! I got to see him play, and he looked GOOD. I mean, he really looked like a skilled player. He made one goal and had three assists. (I think that's how you describe it.) We made eye contact a couple of times. After he made his goal, I jumped up and yelled so loud that everything I was mad about seemed to release itself all in that single yell. I smiled at him, and he gave me the thumbs up.

Mom nudged me and asked if this was an okay Tuesday Time. I gave her a hug and said, "It's the best." For my memory keeper to put in Mom's book, I picked up a small bunch of buttercups. I plan to press them. I'll write a poem or something next to the flowers so this Tuesday Time will go down in HISTORY!

Signed,
Summer, who might have a chance with JASON!!!

P.S. *I haven't told you his full name. Jason Andrew Whitehall. There, you got it! Doesn't it sound good with Summer Ray Whitcomb? Our initials are so close that it's almost freaky. (Okay, not really.)*

August 21

Dear Metti,

I still can't believe I saw Jason play, and he gave me the thumbs up!

I mean, was it to me? No one else was behind me or anything. At least I don't think so. I can be so stupid. I should have turned around and checked. His mom or brother or dad could have been behind me, and he wasn't even seeing me at all! His uncle from Detroit could have been standing behind me, and foolish me thought Jason was looking at me! Now what am I going to do? Why does life have to be so complicated? Why can't I just know for sure that he was looking at me and only me?

Wait; I'll ask my mom when she comes home from work. Yeah, she might have an idea of who was behind us and if Jason was really centering on me. This is so CRAZY!

August 21 (later)

Dear Metti,

Mom says that she wasn't aware of a lot of people behind us. She told me she's pretty sure that Jason had eye contact with me and was not looking into the crowd. I don't know if she is just saying this to help me feel better or if she's for real. Anyway, I have to stay calm and get my thoughts together for a plan before school starts. Just over two weeks left of freedom. Here I come, eighth grade, whether I'm ready for it or not. (NOT!)

Signed,

Summer the soon-to-be eighth-grader

August 23

Dear Metti,

Mom says that since school is starting soon, we'll be doing our Tuesday Time early. She says we're going to the beach for a long weekend. Dad was planning on taking me to the city for two days and an overnight. But here's the shocker—he couldn't get the time off even though he has a bazillion vacation days! See, I live in the suburbs, so going to the city would be awesome. But going to the beach is amazing too.

I'm more of a beach girl anyway. (Can't you tell by my name?) I wish I could wear flip flops all year round. I love wearing just shorts and a t-shirt. I love the water. Any kind of water. Ocean water, pool water, lake water, even rain water. Hey, don't laugh, but I love walking in the rain and splashing in puddles. Did you ever notice how soft your hair is after it dries from being drenched by the rain?

I made my own natural shampoo once. Half of it was made with rain water. The other half was ground-up rose petals, mint leaves, aloe, and beer. It cracks me up that my dad's mom used to tell him to wash his hair once a week with beer to prevent going bald. Guess it worked: Dad isn't bald. Oh, and most importantly, I will be going back to school with an amazing tan! Sun and sand, here I come!

Signed,
Summer, who has to go pack

August 24

Dear Metti,

Isn't it just blissful? Mom and I are sitting on the beach with a perfect breeze to keep us cool. It's low tide, so it's perfect for just sitting and listening. The seagulls are going crazy. Somebody left their bagged lunch, so it's breakfast for the gulls. Mom is nagging me about putting on enough sunscreen. "Summer, you may have the most beautiful name pertaining to nature, but that doesn't make you some sort of goddess who will only tan and not burn. Remember to get your shoulders really good. And you don't want to be burnt on your nose going back to school. Everyone will call you Rudolph."

Anyway, I'm determined to have a good time and put the "nagging mother" out of my mind. Speaking of my mom—she got lost on our way driving down here. Can you believe how crazy she is? Like, we have been coming to this same beach for years! It's only two hours away, but she got all confused and even asked me if we were going in the right direction. My mom needs a VACATION!

August 24 (later)

Dear Metti,

Just came back from a swim. The water was so warm. A lot of cute guys too. There was this one guy—I almost fell into his lap as a wave knocked us both down. Why did it have to be "almost?" Hey, maybe the next time I'll help it along and fall "accidentally" into him.

After supper, Mom said we could go shopping for some cool beach stuff. In this one store, I saw some amazing crop tops. Mom says that I can wear them only over my bathing suit like a swim shirt. But I want to wear them to school (which, of course, I can't because of the dress code). Anyway, if I wear a tank top underneath, then it should be fine for school. I'll just buy one or two.

What I really want to save my money for is a sterling silver dolphin necklace. I eyed it on the first day we got here. It has a crisscross chain with two dolphins arching their necks like they're diving into the water. I totally love it! It will look really nice against my tan. No doubt I'll be wearing it on the first day of school. Oh, school, not yet. I want more summer time.

Signed,
Summer who wants summer.
(Kids tease me about this all the time.)

September 7

Dear Metti,

I can't believe today was the first day of school. It wasn't too bad for someone who isn't the school type. I don't like being inside and talked to all day. I like the hands-on kind of learning. I guess that's why I like science classes where you can do stuff in lab. I like working with my hands. I can hardly wait for Art and Design this semester. I'll get a chance to do some ceramic and textile design and create a 3-D model of my dream home. (That could take me until I graduate! Dream home for real. Like I'll ever be rich enough to afford it. Maybe if Jason becomes a professional soccer player. . .)

Jason and I have third period together, which happens to be math. We also have fifth period together, which happens to be history, and we have the same lunch period. Not much happened today. We saw each other, but that was about it. The first day of school is always so CRAZY! I can't expect much. Hey, at least I have some classes with him.

For my outfit, I did wear my dolphin necklace with one of my new crop tops. (I had a shirt on underneath.) Mrs. Dolson, the school's warden, gave me a warning that my shirt was at the limit of acceptability. She isn't really the school's warden. She's the principal who needs to retire. Anyway, for a first day, it wasn't bad. Except for the food. I think I'll be packing lunch most of the year.

Signed,

Summer the "official" eighth-grader

September 8

Dear Metti,

My mom was pretty sick, so we had to postpone our Tuesday Time. I sure hope I don't get what she had.

I don't know what's up with Jason. I mean, it seemed like we were making a mend over the summer, and now we just glance at one another without saying much. I'm afraid to text him. I don't know what to do. If I do a lot of talking, then I'm afraid I'll scare him off or something.

To top it off—I got my period today. I'm still in the early stages. Mom and the doctor say that I'll get it one month and maybe not again for two months. Google agrees with them, so I believe it. I was lucky I only got it once over the whole summer. It isn't that way for Emily and Racheal. They complain about getting it every month and tell me how they can't do things they want to do because of bad cramps. Whatever. I'm not jealous of that, but I wish my boobs were closer to the sizes of theirs.

Do you think that's why Jason isn't paying much attention to me? I'm not physically mature enough for him? Yeah, he has the build. He really bulked up over the summer.

Signed,
Summer the Boobless

September 10

Dear Metti,

Tonight Mom and I made up for our missed Tuesday Time. I've been kind of depressed about Jason. I know: what's the big deal? I mean, we broke up at the end of the last school year. I should get over it and move on. But then, what about those times over the summer when it seemed like there was hope for us? I mean, I did hear from a reliable source that he still liked me. Right?

Anyway, I told Mom that I just wanted to chill out with some ice cream. Well, as it turned out, we both needed to chill. Mom tries hard to handle "grown-up" problems herself without bringing me into it. Tonight, she needed me as a sounding board, and I wasn't prepared for it. I totally forgot that today is my parent's wedding anniversary. In the years past, both my parents have been cool about it. You know, just another day. I don't remember there being any drama.

Well, there we were, eating our ice cream at one of the outside tables, which was good for me because it wasn't as crowded with people. Without any warning, my mom started to cry. So, I asked her what was wrong. Big mistake! She didn't answer me in words; instead, she started to cry even more. Awkward.

I asked her if she wanted to go home, because that would have been okay with me. She just sat there, crying. Then she started saying stuff about how home isn't what it used to be. I said, "I know." Because of the divorce, I have two homes, but

I'm okay with it. She sobbed about how she doesn't see Forrest much anymore because he lives with Dad. I tried to make light of it, so I told her she was lucky. I have the misfortune of seeing him almost every weekend. Well, that got me a "look" from her. It did interrupt her crying for a second, though.

You see, when Dad and Mom got married, everybody thought that they would change the world together. They were both into keeping the peace, saving the animals, aiding poor countries, and writing books about all their adventures. At first, it was rock and roll for all the good causes. Then Forrest was born, but still things were going strong. Dad was designing pumps to help irrigate drought-stricken areas. Mom was writing a book about animals being slaughtered in the Amazon Rainforest. Thus, how Forrest got his name. They lived a simple life and didn't mind riding to work on bicycles when possible, buying environmentally friendly cars, and being proud owners of the neighborhood's largest compost pile.

Then I was born. I was named after my mom's favorite season. Mom said it was a special time. Dad got promoted to a head engineer's position. Mom was doing great with her writing.

Then, when I was about nine years old, things started getting tense. Dad poured more and more time into his work. He stopped riding his bike and bought a brand-new Mazda. Mom almost had a heart attack. She started getting on his case about polluting the air. He said she was too wrapped up in her causes, and he needed to do what he felt was best for himself. Back and forth it went.

When I had just turned 11, they got a divorce. Forrest lived with Mom and me for a while, but he went to live with Dad when he started college. Mom never did finish her book about the Amazon Rainforest.

For my Tuesday Time memento, I saved a napkin from the ice cream place and wrote a note on it. "I'll be your anniversary date anytime."

So there you have it. Pretty much the whole story of my life. Yep, the whole Whitcomb family story. Got to go to bed. There's school tomorrow, and I can't fall asleep in math class. I have to be awake to see Jason.

Nite Nite,
Summer, who knows a thing or
two about her family

September 11

Dear Metti,

I just don't know what to do about Jason. Today in math class, he looked so serious. I tried to make eye contact with him, but he just kept his head down, staring at his desk. I wish I knew what was going on with him. I don't need to know the details, though that would be nice. I just need to know if he is okay or not. I mean, maybe he is really sick with some kind of disease. Maybe, or not, he broke up with a new girlfriend. Or maybe, someone close in his family is really sick, or worse yet, died. I don't know if I could ever go back to school if my mom or my dad or even Forrest died.

My grandmother on Mom's side is still living. She's 87 years old, but you wouldn't think so by how active she is. She lives in the Willow Grove Retirement Community. She plays shuffleboard like nobody's business.

All my other grandparents are dead. I never knew my grandfather on my dad's side. He died when my dad was eight years old. Back then, it was hard for a single mother with four children to find a job and survive. My dad is the oldest of his family, and he vowed he would take care of them. He got his first job at ten, delivering newspapers. In his teen years, he worked at a bowling alley and mowed the lawns of his high school. To this day, my mom speaks highly about my dad being a hard worker and a very good provider for those he cares for. My child support check never comes late. But what went wrong, according to my mom, is how the hard work became my dad's sole focus. His working so hard to provide is what actually broke up the family.

I really do know how to ramble. I'll come up with a plan for Jason. I just need time to think about it. It's times like these that I wish I had a big sister. If I had it my way, I would have an older sister and a younger brother. Yep, I would LOVE to be the boss of a younger brother.

Signed,
Summer the rambler

September 14

Dear Metti,

Today in math class, I really didn't have a plan as to how I was going to get Jason's attention. So I did something I rarely do for fear of getting caught and losing my phone. But I took the risk and texted Jason. I just asked how he was doing if that was okay with him. But then I had to turn my head toward Mr. Morland because I had a hunch he was going to ask me to answer a question. Sure enough, he did, and I didn't slip up. How bad that would have been if I screwed up my answer in front of everybody, including Jason. Math is my best subject. I like math a lot. I mean, people know this about me. I can still ace a test without studying for it.

Jason didn't look toward me at all. At the end of class, I tried to get his attention with a small wave, but he rushed out of the room before I had a chance. We have the same lunch period and the same history class at the end of the day. I'll keep an open mind about it. I haven't even seen him talking in the halls with his soccer buddies. Something just isn't right. I have to find out somehow. I know that I'm not his girlfriend anymore, but I still care. I mean, we could maybe become friends. Or not.

Signed,
Summer (wrote this during study hall)

September 14

Dear Metti,

Nothing happened during lunch period except for the monthly food fight. The "whoevers" of the school always have a food fight to show how it's their tradition to put noodles in someone's hair. They get caught, go to ISS (which is In-School Suspension), and then days later they're back at it again. For the most part, this group is harmless. They dress a bit differently—like goths. You know: all black in long coats with heavy combat boots, and the girls wear dark makeup with licorice-shaded lipstick.

During history class, Jason passed me a note saying there was stuff going on, and he would tell me later. Now, my curiosity is seriously getting the best of me. Later means like how much later? Will he text me tonight, or do I have to wait until he tells me at school? Oh, but he did write back to me!!! I guess all I can do is wait.

Signed,
Summer, who is NOT good at waiting!

September 14 (later)

Dear Metti,

I couldn't sleep, so I thought of a better idea: to spill out my thoughts rather than keep tossing around in bed fighting to keep them inside my head.

I can't stop thinking about Jason. Metti, you never had the chance to meet him, so let me tell you about him. I still like him. Okay, that says nothing about him. Jason, oh, Jason. For starters, he looks like a Jason. Which happens to be a name I really like. A Jason looks sturdy. Jason is sturdy. A Jason smiles just enough not to overwhelm the rest of his face. Jason has this classic sheepish smile. Jasons aren't lazy. Jason is not lazy. I know I complain about how his life is all soccer, but I see now how it's his passion, not something he used to avoid me. Jasons are quiet. Jason is quiet, but he knows when to speak up and be heard for what he feels is important to be shared. Jason can talk quite a bit in history class. He gets into debates with the teacher and other students. Jason has definite opinions, and he isn't shy about expressing them.

I guess that's one of the main reasons I like him. I know where he stands. He doesn't have a flip-floppy kind of personality. Jason is strong. And I guess that's what's bothering me. Right now, Jason doesn't look very strong. He looks like he's being choked by his own emotions. Metti, he isn't acting himself. I miss the old Jason.

Signed,
Summer, who sounds like an expert on all Jasons. (Well, maybe just one.)

42

September 15

Dear Metti,

   Still no news from Jason. That's the bad news. The good news is that today is Tuesday, and Mom and I did something. This is good because it will help keep my mind off of Jason. It's my pick, so we're going to RayMon's Bowling Alley. Because it's a school night, we have to leave as soon as Mom gets home from work at about 5:15(ish). She wanted me to make sandwiches for supper to save a bit of money. But I told her I had homework to get done. No homework, but I'm counting my writing as a work in progress. So I didn't totally lie. RayMon's has the best burgers and fries. What can I say? A girl has to eat. Got to go. Write more to you later.

Signed,
Summer,
who's cravin' burgers and fries

September 15

Dear Metti,

It's kind of late, but I just had to put it in writing: I bowled my best game EVER!!! I beat my mom by five points. We played two out of three games was the winner, and the loser had to get the winner anything she wanted from the snack bar. Seeing that I won. . . I got more french fries. At first, Mom was winning with some easy strikes. Then I pulled up.

We all used to bowl a lot before the divorce. In fact, both Mom and Dad were on a bowling league. I even attended a few bowling camps. I guess you could say that we had the lanes in our veins.

For my Tuesday Time souvenir, I'm keeping the printout of the score sheet. Who knows? Maybe I'll go out for the bowling team when I'm in high school.

Signed,
Summer the Strike Queen

September 16

Dear Metti,

Still no news from Jason. Actually, he was absent from school today. So no chance to get a note from him. Still waiting, but getting more concerned.

Speaking of concerned, today my mom did something she never does: missed a meeting. In all my years of knowing my mom and how she does her job, she has never, I mean never, missed a meeting. And today she came home from work looking pale and out of it. So I asked her what was wrong. That's when she told me in this robot tone that she missed a meeting scheduled for 2:00 this afternoon. I tried to lighten up her mood by saying it was all because I beat her in bowling, and her world is so rocked that she can't concentrate. Well, that didn't go over very well.

You need to know something about my mom. She takes her job very seriously. She doesn't forget. Even when she's sick, she doesn't forget. My mom is a free spirit through and through, but when it comes to her day-to-day life, she is organized to the point of labeling "organization" itself. She can go off to Mexico on an hour's notice, but she's all organized in how she gets there.

I told her that she's fine. There's nothing to be concerned about. I asked her if she got in trouble for not being at the meeting. She said no, because everyone was in such a shock that she didn't show. They couldn't imagine her not ever showing up. Well, that was a good thing. If I didn't show up for a class because I forgot, I would be in trouble and then some. Just the same, it was weird of my mom. She's been acting so ditzy lately. I hope everything is okay. Like, I hope she doesn't have brain cancer or something.

Signed,
Summer the exaggerator

September 17

Dear Metti,

No word from Jason. Still hoping. Still waiting.

Signed,
Summer in a slump

September 18

Dear Metti,

Jason finally texted me back about wanting to talk. He didn't want to talk at school, so we took a long walk around town. At first I was all jumpy inside. I was excited, nervous, happy, and overall hyper. I had been waiting for us to be able to talk for like forever, and now it was finally happening. So as quietly as I could, I took deep breaths, while inside my head I shouted, "SUMMER, YOU BETTER BE COOL!"

Jason was mellow. It seemed like a depressed kind of mellow rather than a chill kind of mellow. At points we were walking shoulder-to-shoulder because a skater would whizz by us on the sidewalk. I certainly didn't mind our shoulders touching.

Stores on Main Street were still open. I asked if Jason wanted to buy a snack at the Stop In store. He said he wasn't in the mood to eat anything. I played it smooth and said I wasn't much in the mood for food either. Then, Jason started the serious talking.

First, he said, "Well, sorry for not getting back to you. And for kind of ignoring you. I didn't really mean it like that."

I said that it was okay. But inside I was screaming, "I was a nervous wreck, wondering what was wrong!" I played it cool, I think. Anyway, I think he still likes me, but not in the way I would like him to like me. Make sense? He just needed someone to talk to as a friend. I'm fine with that.

It was hard for him to tell me what's been going on. While

we were dating, I didn't know much about his family life. I met his mom and dad, and they're nice. I met his older brother a few times in passing. The stuff Jason told me had to do with his older brother, Brad.

Brad still lives at home because he's going to a community college. Well, as Jason puts it: he isn't just getting a degree in accounting. He's also getting a degree in drinking. Brad has been pulled over a bunch and gotten three DUIs.

Up to this point, nothing very serious has happened. The first time, he was swaying in and out of the lane. A cop saw it and pulled him over. Second time, he drove through a stop sign, thankfully not crashing into anyone. The third time, he smashed into a parked car in the college parking lot. The car he hit happened to have a student sitting in it, waiting for his girlfriend to get out of class. Again, no one was hurt.

Then came a fourth time, and Brad got arrested with no questions asked. He was driving home from drinking at a bar and ran a red light. He crashed into another car. This time, people got hurt. The car he hit had a mom and daughter in it. Both of them had to be flown to the hospital. They're okay. But the dad/husband of the family he hit is suing Brad for everything he's worth. And the police aren't going easy on him, either.

Police-wise, Brad's facing five to seven years in jail. After that, a year of house arrest. Then two years of probation. Chances are he will lose his driver's license for good.

Jason is really down. Brad's a pretty good soccer player. Jason always looked up to him. In fact, it was Brad who taught Jason most of what he knows about soccer. They would spend hours in their backyard doing dribbling drills. Jason feels as though his world has shattered like a snow globe. I asked him when Brad goes to jail. He said around Thanksgiving time.

I didn't know what to say or what to do. So, like an idiot, I just kept walking without saying anything. Jason seemed okay with it. But I felt really awkward. Then it got even more awkward. Jason started to get mad. He started cursing. He picked up rocks and threw them at random targets. After he vented some, we sat on a bench. He started to cry a bit. Then, I don't know what came over me, but I held his hand. It wasn't the hand-holding like I want others to notice, "Hey, I'm with Jason." You know, like, "Look at us we're a couple." Not like that. It was the kind of hand-holding you do when a friend doesn't feel good, is going through some painful stuff, or is moving away from you. At the time, it just seemed like the thing I was supposed to do to help him.

After some silence, which seemed louder than my pounding heart, I finally whispered to him that I was so sorry, and if there was anything I could do to just let me know. He whispered back that I had already helped by just being there for him to talk to. We walked back toward home in more silence, our hands crumpled in our pockets. When we got back to my house, Jason said goodbye. He walked away, kicking stones like he was doing soccer drills with his brother. I feel really guilty now for being so jealous about Jason loving soccer more than me.

Jason has some tough times ahead of him. But you know what? I'm not even thinking of getting back together. I just want to be a friend who can hold his hand, letting him know that somehow, someway, it's going to be okay.

Signed,
Summer the emotionally exhausted

September 22

Dear Metti,

Today, Mom and I had our Tuesday Time. I think I did a most horrible thing. I get so mad at myself for talking too much. I can have such a big mouth. I think you know where I'm going with this.

Mom and I decided to stay home, eat delivery pizza, and watch a movie. Well, we got the staying home and eating pizza part done. But not the movie. We were sitting on a big picnic blanket, chowing down on our pizza, when I just blurted out how I have a friend who is going through a rough time. I hinted that I needed advice on how to help this particular friend.

You know parents: "Is this friend into drinking, smoking pot, or taking drugs?" And it went on. "Is this friend pregnant?"

Oh my gosh! Mom has to chill out. I told her that it wasn't anything affecting my friend directly. It was someone in my friend's family that's causing trouble. And just like that, she asked, "What's going on with Jason's family?" How did she know so soon into our conversation? She said she read about it in the local newspaper. Of course! My mom will be reading after she's dead. I asked her why she hadn't mentioned it to me. She said that she wanted me to find out personally through Jason if it was something that Jason wanted others to know.

I told her that I felt better knowing that I didn't have to officially tell her because she had read it in the paper. I'm not one for gossip. She asked me how I was dealing with the news.

I told her I was okay. Then she asked how Jason was taking it. And that's when I got watery eyes. I told her that Jason was not very well. He seems shut down and distant. She reached over and gave me a hug. We just sat close to each other, talking about simple stupid stuff compared to what the talk must be in Jason's house. No matter what, I'm going to be there for Jason.

I couldn't imagine what it would be like if Forrest did something like this. I guess my older brother isn't so bad after all. I guess its times like these that you become grateful for what you have instead of what you don't have. From now on, I'm going to try to focus on what I have. Really, my life isn't bad at all. I mean, at least I won't be visiting any one of my family members in jail. Oh, what if Jason wants me to go with him someday to visit Brad in jail? I've never been to a jail. I guess I have some time to think about it.

I got to sign off. School tomorrow, and I'm really tired.

Signed,
Summer the Grateful

P.S. *For my Tuesday Time keepsake, I wrote on a tissue about how Mom and I talked about Brad going to jail. (I did cry.)*

September 24

Dear Metti,

Not much to write about today. There's one thing, though, that I need to share with you. My mom came home from work and put her keys on the key ring holder right inside the front door. Like, she does this every day of her life. Nothing new, right? She went down into the basement to put clothes in the dryer. Then, she came back up asking me if I'd seen her keys. It was weird.

Then it got weirder. I said, "Mom, you know exactly where your keys are. You put them in the same place every day of your life." She gave me this blank look that lasted for five long seconds. Then she laughed it off, walking out of the kitchen like she was going through a maze. Minutes later, I heard her shout, "So this is where my keys went!"

I swear I think she forgot where the front door was. Well, at least where she put her keys. My mom is an excessively organized freak. She would never in a million years forget where she puts her keys! I don't know. Call me crazy, but I think my mom is going CRAZY!!!

Signed,
Summer, the daughter
of a crazy mother

September 27

Dear Metti,

Sorry for not writing in a couple days. Life has been busy with schoolwork. I'm not at all into school like some kids who would go year 'round if they could. But I'm not against school either, like those who go from class to class carrying nothing but pencils in their back pockets. I'm your average semi-school-loving kid who has the average grades to go with it. So when there are reports to do or science projects, I can get into it.

These past few days, I was busy writing a report for history class. I did my report on the Prohibition of the 1920s. The 1920s were known as the roaring '20s because of the crime caused by the mob vs. a failed justice system vs. parties with flapper girls. My mom showed me some popular dance moves of the '20s and dances like the Charleston, the Twist, and the Fox Trot. "Weird," was all I said after she showed me. This was all before my mom's time. But my great-grandmother could tell you some interesting stories growing up in the 1920s.

My great-grandmother on my dad's side was born in 1904. She was a waitress for a popular dance hall called The Nightingale. She had an exciting life, if you ask me. She said that, before some of the famous got famous, they would perform at the "Gale," as the regulars would call it. Such performers as Billy Holiday, Erle Hinez, and Louie Armstrong played there. Since it was the Prohibition, most people couldn't sell alcohol, but that law didn't stop some of the big-timers. What I mean is the mob. Oh, the mob was vicious back then. If you crossed one of their top players, you could be certain your number was up. You would be killed, usually in a pretty painful way. The mob wanted to make a statement that said: You mess with us, you die a messy death.

As you can see, I had some interest in doing this report. My Great-Grandma Roxanna was married to my Great-Grandpa George, who was a police officer for their town. He got shot by a woman who was trying to hide her family's bootlegging business. Roxie (which became her nickname as soon as she started dating my grandfather) would say that this was the hardest part of his job: when women pointed their guns at him. Women figured a policeman wouldn't have the courage to shoot a woman because he should be too much of a gentleman. Great-Grandpa George couldn't shoot back. It cost him his life.

Years later, I found out that Great-Grandma Roxie carried a boot pistol. She said that she talked it over with George's spirit, and they had an understanding between them that she needed some sense of safety. Times were getting rough. More and more smuggling was going on. Men, women, and even children were getting killed because of the war between the smugglers and the law.

It's getting late. I practically wrote a new report here. I guess I'm starting to think of myself as a writer. Never in a trillion years did I think that would be true. I guess life can be full of surprises. Speaking of surprises: Mom said that our Tuesday Time is going to be a surprise. I hope it's as good as the last time she surprised me!

Signed,
Summer, the family historian

55

September 28

Dear Metti,

Jason said that the court cases his brother has to go to are so unpredictable. The court says one thing and then changes it the next time the lawyers meet.

Some days I forget about it. Life just gets too busy with stuff. But I know that isn't the case for Jason and his family. Life is never too busy for them to forget.

Signed,
Summer, who is sad

P.S. *Wrote this during English class.*

September 28

Dear Metti,

Remember a couple of days ago when I told you I thought my mom was going crazy? Well, something happened again. My mom is the most organized person in the world, so it's kind of scaring me that she is forgetting stuff. There is a "mail station" in our house. This mail station is very important to my mother. Especially since the divorce, she totally relies on this sacred area of the house like her very life depends on it. I mean this literally. She is so nervous about losing a bill, missing a payment, or sending a payment out late. So like, forever, since I can remember, she's had a mail station in each of the three houses we've lived in. The mail station consists of clearly labeled bins arranged in order of importance. The first bin is the "Monthly Bills" bin. This bin has the bills that need to be paid on a monthly basis like the house payment, the electric, the car, and my lunch account. Then there is the "Non-Monthly Bills" bin. Bills like trash, sewer, and other stuff. Then there is the "Correspondence" bin. Lastly, there's the "Junk" mail bin. Junk mail is like your store ads and coupons. You know, stuff like that.

So last night, she asked me if I'd seen the car payment bill. This was weird in and of itself. My parents have never asked me about the status of their bills. But I went with it and told her to check the mail station. And she said, "Oh, honey, I think they're closed."

I said, "Mom, you know, our mail station."

"Such a silly girl," she replied, "thinking we have our very own post office right here at home."

I was so close to yelling at her as I walked over to the mail station shelf and pointed right at it. Then I heard her mumbling it again that it wouldn't be open this late at night.

I froze in my tracks. I mean, I just froze. I stood there staring at her with my mouth opened as wide as a canning jar.

I asked her if she was feeling okay. She said yes. She didn't look drunk to me, but I asked her anyway if she was drunk. She laughed it off, saying that she hadn't had a drink since meeting my dad's new boss. Whatever that means, and whenever that was.

I'm totally freaked out! I gently excused myself by telling her I was going for a walk. She said okay, and that was that. She went into the kitchen to empty the dishwasher. I would have written to you earlier, but I was so nervous about it all.

I hope this is just a side effect to menopause. I know my mom is old enough to be going through it. I think I'll do some research on it. Weird, weird, weird! I'm researching stuff about my own mother.

Signed,
Summer the freaked-out daughter

September 29

Dear Metti,

Here it is: Tuesday again. We decided to lay low for our Tuesday Time. One of the things my mom and I have in common is our love for breakfast food. So we pigged out on waffles, scrambled eggs, and cold cereal of our choice. WE LOVED IT!!! Breakfast for supper all the way! (I'm still sticky from the syrup.)

Signed,
Summer, also known as "Sticky Fingers"

September 30

Dear Metti,

Today is my brother's birthday. Forrest is 21 years old. He is a bit older than other college sophomores because he repeated first grade. He kept that a secret for years. He was totally embarrassed and ashamed that he had to repeat a grade in school. It was mostly because Mom and Dad moved out-of-district right in the middle of the school year. Forrest never really caught up in the new school so the teacher and my parents thought it was best for him to repeat first grade. Oh, there have been times when he got me so MAD that I yelled at him, "At least I didn't have to repeat first grade!" One day, when I said that, he just about killed me! Forrest is a geek god. Everything revolves around grades, education, honors, and being in the top ten percent of his class.

Mom and I sang Happy Birthday to him over the phone. We'll be seeing him on Saturday to celebrate. After Mom was done talking to him, I called him back so I could talk to him. I didn't know how to start because Forrest and I never really talk. I mean, we hang out and talk about movies, our favorite fast food restaurants, and the little we know about sports. But a deep conversation—never.

My attack was simple: "Forrest, I'm freaking out about Mom. She's doing some weird stuff, and I need you to know about it."

My brother replied, "Shoot, kiddo, I'm all ears."

"Come again? Did I hear you right?"

"Yeah, Summer, I have some time to listen. After all, it's my birthday, so I can do whatever I want. Right?"

"Yeah, yeah, it's your birthday."

I don't remember exactly what I said then. All I know is that an hour and fifteen minutes later, I felt much better. I told Forrest about Mom missing her meeting. Then how she lost her car keys in the house. And then the biggie! How she thought that the mail station was somewhere outside of our house.

Forrest told me to take a breath. He did agree with me that those things aren't like Mom at all. I told him I would keep an eye on her. I told him that I intend to research menopause effects in women. He thought that was a good place to start.

Then I think I entered another realm of life. My brother, Forrest, said that he was glad that I had talked to him, and if I get worried over other stuff to give him a call! I told him that would be fine—"And wow, are you feeling alright?" He laughed, and we said our goodbyes.

I'm shocked. I'm stunned. I'm mystified. Well, whatever has gotten into Forrest. . . stay there, if it means this kind of change in him.

Signed,
Summer, who really
does have a BROTHER

October 3

Dear Metti,

Today, Mom and I celebrated with Forrest for his birthday.
WELL, WELL, WELL! Remember how I wrote that whatever
has gotten into my brother can stay? Well, what's going on
with my brother is. . . FORREST has a girlfriend! YES! Mr.
Geek God has a geek goddess. Her name is Clara Rose Weston.
She is a year younger than Forrest, but you wouldn't know
it. She acts pretty mature. She talks about books, science, and
current events, and she's funny. She has this spark about her
that bursts out in a sort of quietly intense manner and makes
you laugh. Her brown hair is shoulder length with strong red
highlights. She was wearing glasses because her contacts were
being ordered. Her eyes match the brown tone in her hair. She
stands at Forrest's biceps. (He is rather tall, and she is kind of
short.)

Anyway, she joined us for ice cream cake at Dairy Land. But
she asked first to be sure it was okay with us. I liked that about
her the most. She hasn't planted her stake in Forrest's life yet
as if claiming him for herself. We had a good time. But Mom
seemed lost at times. Like there was this lost puppy look on her
face. I don't think Forrest noticed because he was so nervously
happy about us being okay with Clara Rose. Maybe it was just
a bit much for Mom. You know, with Forrest turning a year
older and finding his first "serious" girlfriend, which could lead
to marriage and grandchildren.

Oh, I could be in their wedding! Jason could see me all dressed up and mature looking! And when Mom and Dad become grandparents, I'll become an aunt!!!

Yeah, this is going too far even for me. I'm just happy for Forrest. I mean, I'm really happy for Forrest. Clara Rose seems to be a good fit for him. I know that I just met her for the first time. But I have a good feeling about her. Yeah, a good feeling. My overly smart brother better not do something stupid and break up with her. If ever there was a smart thing for my brother to do, it would be to stick with this girl. She's a keeper.

Signed,
Summer, who dreams that she'll
someday be an aunt

October 6

Dear Metti,

   Our Tuesday Time was today. It was a joint idea as to what to do. We hadn't been to the mall for pretzels in a long time, so off we went. It all started because the weather was a bit chilly, and that set off the idea in both of our heads for getting pretzels. There's this place in the mall called Pretzels with a Twist that make these amazing pretzels! They make pretzels out of uniquely flavored dough. Our favorite happens to be pumpkin. And they only have pumpkin during October and November. So we licked our fingers with salted pumpkin glaze that never tasted better! We topped our treat off with pumpkin spice tea. For my memento, I saved a napkin and wrote on it, "We want pumpkin pretzels ALL THE TIME!"

Signed,

Summer, the pumpkin pretzel eater

October 9

Dear Metti,

I really don't know what to do. Yesterday was such a perfect fall day, with the weather starting to change and eating the "to die for" pretzels at the mall. Forrest has a girlfriend, and it just seems like things around me are changing for the better.

Well, it turns out not all things are getting better. My mom is really beginning to freak me out. I came home from school today and, like normal, she wasn't home from work yet. No big deal, until suddenly it was 7:30, and she still wasn't home.

She gets off at 5:00. But normally that means 5:30 by the time she finalizes everything. The drive home is fifteen minutes, max. There isn't any traffic to get stuck in because it's all residential roads. So, at 7:45 I called her cell phone. When no one answered, I started to get really worried.

I texted her: Where r u?

I called the library to be sure she hadn't gotten held up with some irate patron. (Oh, yes, library patrons can act like jerks, all because of a library fine.)

No, she wasn't at the library, and they told me that she had left at 5:20. The staff person tried to keep me calm by making suggestions, like maybe Mom had stopped for gas, was running some errands, or was picking up dinner—"I'm sure she'll be bringing it home any time now."

Well, that wasn't the case. I called her cell phone about a hundred more times. No answer. At 8:50, I called again to be sure she hadn't gone back to the library because she had forgotten something. No, she hadn't been seen since she left.

I called Forrest, but he didn't answer. This was the wrong time to forward my calls. I sent him a text, then another:

Forrest please call me, Mom's missing
Call me now!!!!!!!!!!!!!!!

I called Mrs. Lentz, our very old but very helpful neighbor, who we have known for years. She detected how upset I was getting, so she told me that if Mom wasn't home by 9:30 to come over to her house.

Then, at 9:10, Mom showed up. The front door opened, and there stood my mom. She looked awful! I ran up to her and hugged her so tight. Then a big wave of fear just totally crashed down on me. I told her how worried I'd been—no, how scared I'd been—and where had she been, anyhow? Why didn't she call or text me to let me know she was alright?

My mom just stood there like a melting icicle. She stood cold and stiff, yet gave me a warm and gentle hug. Finally, she told me about her evening, talking in a strange, small voice. The whole time she spoke, I couldn't believe what she was saying. It was like a very bad joke.

This is what happened: after Mom left the library, she went to Big Nate's meat store to pick up fresh pork chops for dinner. Then she thought how nice it would be to have freshly baked rolls from Lily Tye's bakery. She said all was going well until she realized she didn't know her way home from the bakery. This is why she didn't call or text me: because she was driving here, there, and everywhere trying to get home. I asked her how she got lost. She just shrugged. Then I asked her how she got home. She must have figured it out, because here she is.

"Summer, I got so frustrated and scared and angry. How stupid of me to get lost! So I pulled off the road and cried. While I was sitting there, a police car drove up behind me. Sure enough, an officer walked over to my car. He tapped on my window. So I rolled my window down, thinking I was going to get a ticket for illegal parking. But instead he asked me if everything was alright. I said yes, I was fine. But no, because I'm lost. Summer, I got lost in my own neighborhood. In my own stupid neighborhood! The police officer had to give me directions so I could find my way back to my own home! I couldn't even remember to try GPS until I was almost back." By this point we both were crying. Crying because we were scared. Scared that what she was telling me, and what I was hearing, was real. Very real; too real.

My mother. My strong, intellectual, independent, self-assured mother felt so frail in my arms as I helped her into the living room so we could just sit and hold each other on the couch. Oh, Metti, I just kept crying. I didn't know what to say, how to respond, or how to help us both to feel better. After a bit, I went into the kitchen to make us some tea. I stood over the tea kettle, letting the steam blend in with my tears.

Inside, bubbling up, was a very thick fear. Was my mother losing her mind? Was she fighting a life-threatening illness? Brain cancer?

I felt like I was drowning in a darkness of unknowns. But what I know now is that we need to get some answers. I'll start by talking to Forrest when he calls back. No, better yet I'll meet him for lunch. I have to talk to him in person.

I finished making up a tea tray with cheese and crackers. When I walked back into the living room, Mom had fallen asleep. There she lay like a child, so trusting that she was now somewhere safe, regardless of what had happened. I put a blanket on her and left the tea tray on the kitchen table. I came upstairs to my room to confide in you, Metti, everything that has happened, only to find myself crying all over again.

Signed,
Summer, who is afraid

October 10

Dear Metti,

Today is Saturday! Thank goodness. Plus, it's a Saturday that Mom doesn't have to work, and I don't have to go to my dad's because he's away on business. Mom and I both slept in this morning. I think we got wiped out from last night.

When I went downstairs to check on Mom, she wasn't on the couch, in the kitchen, or in the downstairs den. I poked my head out the front door. There she was, raking leaves out of our flower bed. She looked up at me with this bright sparkle in her eye and an even brighter smile on her face. She said good morning in a way only Mom does: "Hey, sweetie. What's kickin', chicken?"

It was as if nothing had ever happened. I am officially freaked out a hundred times over! I don't know what to do. I didn't know if she was just pretending so I wouldn't be worried, or if she really had forgotten all of last night.

Should I say something to her? You know, to see how she responds. Or should I just go with the flow and wait until she says something about it to me?

I'll be calling Forrest later today. This isn't the kind of thing I can just text him. He did finally text me late last night to make sure everything was okay, but by then Mom was asleep on the couch and I was out cold in bed. He couldn't talk this morning; he had a crash course today. What a way to spend your Saturday. He's in class for six hours so he can graduate with an added certificate to his degree. I won't be going to college. You couldn't pay me enough to spend six hours on a Saturday trying to learn something!

Signed,
Summer, who is taking
one day at a time

October 11

Dear Metti,

Well, I finally got a hold of Forrest. He didn't get home until 10:30 last night. He said he was pretty tired. What the heck? He didn't brush me off and tell me to call him tomorrow. Something is up with him, and I guess it's the power of a girlfriend.

At first, I stumbled for words to tell him. That soon changed, because within five minutes of our conversation's start, I was sobbing all over the place. In short, I was a mess. We talked for almost two hours. It was a good talk. I feel better knowing that I can keep Forrest up-to-date with what's going on with Mom. Yet I feel kind of bad for my mom at the same time. It kind of feels like we're ganging up on her. You know, her son and daughter talking about her behind her back.

Forrest was quiet in the beginning. But he got more talkative as we kept on chatting. He asked if I could casually talk to any of my friends to see if anyone in their family is acting confused. If so, maybe they would have some advice. I told him about my friends Emily and Rachel. But they are pretty busy with school sports. This isn't the easiest topic to bring up for advice.

But I think I want to keep this more private. I would feel more comfortable with the idea of talking to someone who doesn't know Mom. All of my friends know her. I didn't mention Jason. I wasn't going to go there.

I asked Forrest if he was worried about Mom. He was silent for a bit then said that he was. I asked him in what way was he worried, and he said he wanted to tell me more in person. So we are meeting next Saturday, the 17th. This works out good because Mom works that Saturday. Throughout our conversation, Forrest kept asking me if I was okay. Whoa!!! He's totally rocking my world. What's happening to my brother? Never mind. It's all good by me.

Signed,
Summer, the Little Sis

October 13

Dear Metti,

Thank goodness it isn't Friday the 13th. I'm not into that kind of stuff, but 13 can seem like a scary number. I've been thinking about what Forrest said to me the other day when I called him. He seemed like he was protecting me from something. Like there was more for him to tell me, but he was holding it back from me. I know he said that he would tell me more in person. But I still have this feeling like a bomb is waiting to explode, when I think it's only as serious as some gunshots. The gunshot when Mom missed her meeting. The gunshot when she lost her car keys. But that horrible night when she didn't come home, like forever—that was more like a bomb.

I've also been thinking about how Forrest thought it was important for me to have a friend to casually confide in. Well, I know what you're thinking. Maybe, just maybe, since Jason is going through rough times with his brother Brad, MAYBE, we could go through tough times together. You know, be support for each other because we each have stuff to deal with and work through. You know, like "two peas in a pod." What do you think? Good idea or not such a good idea?

Yeah, I agree: I need to take some time to think about it. I don't want to blow it with him. Trust is like a brick that you don't want to blindly throw through a glass window.

Lately, I just haven't been able to think about how my friends would handle all this scary stuff that's going on with my mom.

Maybe it's the same way with Jason? We see each other and say "hi." We still talk at lunch when we sit together. But no real conversation since he told me about his brother. I just have this knot in my gut that it's going to be okay, but in a hard kind of way. It's going to be okay, but it's going to be hard dealing with the fact that your brother is in jail for several years. Brad's going to have a record for the rest of his life. And I think Jason feels like he's going to be the younger brother of a "criminal" for the rest of his life. Once word gets out in school, who knows what it's going to be like?

Signed,

Summer, who feels for Jason

October 14

Dear Metti,

Oh snap, I got writing to you so much about my mom that I forgot to write about our Tuesday Time, which was yesterday. We didn't do anything but play some card games. It did get interesting, though, when my mom thought it was a good idea to teach me how to play poker. Not just how to play the cards but how to place the bets to win. I didn't know this about my mom, but apparently she was a bit of a poker player in her day. She claims that's how Forrest is getting through college: with all her winnings. (I don't believe her.) April Whitcomb: a Serious Poker Player isn't what comes to my mind when I think of my mother. We listened to the song "The Gambler" by Kenny Rogers while gambling on bite-sized chocolate bars. (They're almost gone, so we have to buy more for Halloween.)

You know, my mom's okay. She's been doing some weird things lately. But then score, I found out she was a poker queen in her day. Sweet! For the scrapbook memento, I'm gluing a poker chip to the page.

Signed,
Summer, who's takin'
a gamble. (Get it?)

October 16

Dear Metti,

I went to our school's Friday night football game. What school in the whole United States doesn't have Friday night football? I was walking around, looking for somebody to sit with, when I got a blow. I mean a BIG BLOW! I saw this girl Carolynne and her friend Elizabeth sitting in the stands. I know them both from my math and science classes. We waved at each other, and they motioned for me to sit with them. As I started walking up the stairs, I saw Jason sitting with Megan Parker. And I mean sitting next to each other! There wasn't any space between them! For a split second, Jason looked at me, and then he turned away. I played it cool. I went to sit with Carolynne and Elizabeth. As I sat down, I demanded the stinging tears to go away.

By the third quarter, my emotions got the best of me. I told them I had to go. I lied a bit and said that I had to get up early to babysit tomorrow. As I walked down the bleachers, Jason was getting up. The worst timing in the universe. He walked down the stairs three people behind me. At the bottom of the stairs, he grabbed my arm.

"Sorry for not telling you," he said. The sound of his voice made my heart race!

I shot him a look that said it all—"You're not sorry." I pulled away and marched out of the stadium. I didn't call my mom to come pick me up. I needed the time and space to be alone, so I walked. I cried on the outside, while inside my head I screamed all sorts of nasty things at Jason. But mostly I cried. Over and over, I kept thinking, "Why is my life going so crazy?" I wanted to scream really loud. So I did! And then I ran home.

Signed,
Summer, who feels like she's losing SOMETHING!

October 17

Dear Metti,

   I woke up this morning seriously not in a good mood. All I
wanted to do was stay in bed, buried under my covers like an
angry, hurt bear. But even though it's the weekend, I had to
get up so Mom would go to work so Forrest and I can meet for
lunch without her knowing about it. Something inside of me
just wants to hug my big brother. I'll be back later to write all
about it. Wish me luck that our "brother-sister talk" goes well.

Signed,
Summer, who's signing off for now

October 17 (later)

Dear Metti,

We pulled it off: Forrest and I met for lunch without Mom knowing about it. It comes in handy that she works every second Saturday of the month. Before I give you any of the details of our meeting—I'll spare you from the suspense and tell you that our conversation went fine. Let's just say that it went better than I would have imagined. (Big brother even paid for my lunch.)

At first, we were focused on what we wanted to eat. I guess we both were anxious and hungry for some restaurant food. Forrest got the Super Burger Combo, and I got the Saturday Breakfast Special. (I order breakfast food any chance I get.) My idea of comfort food is a bowl of cereal. Forrest's comfort food is a hamburger, the bigger the better. After he ordered his coffee, he gave me a nod, allowing me to order coffee too. There was something so rewarding about the two of us sitting there, sipping on our coffees while engaged in a grownup conversation. I don't remember ever having a time like this, where I felt mature enough to fit inside my brother's world.

I started the talking. You know, the small talk first. He showed interest in me by small-talking back. Then our food came. It helped our talking to have food to munch on. Forrest made eye contact with me through the steam of his coffee, and in a rather serious tone asked me how Mom was doing. His tone and eye contact intimidated me a bit. But I didn't slink down into the "I'm-just-the-little-sister what-do-I-know?" shyness. Maybe it was the coffee, but I felt more confident inside. I felt a connection rather than feeling a thousand years apart!

I told him how Mom is really beginning to scare me. I recapped how she missed a meeting at work. I told him everything all over again. All the while I was talking, he really held his attention on me. I told him how she gets disoriented in her very own house. I told him how she gets confused with her driving directions.

I told him how I looked up symptoms of menopause to see if that was what was going on with her. Yeah, it stated that a woman's memory can be challenged during this time. Forgetfulness is a common aspect to it, but not on the same level as Mom. It didn't mention intense confusion with normal, everyday tasks. Forgetfulness during menopause is more like just being scatterbrained. You eventually remember what you were forgetting. Your memory can be jogged. It may be hours later, but your memory can bring it up for you to remember.

I told Forrest that what I was witnessing was different from what they described. Mom doesn't remember, period. Hours later, or even the next day, her memory doesn't bring it back for her to remember.

I told him about the horrible time she came home in the dead of night because she got lost coming home from Lily Tye's bakery. I told him how she had to get directions from a police officer to get home. I described how she looked totally awful.

At this point, Forrest looked shocked. He told me it was the right thing to do in calling him, texting him, whatever was needed to get in touch with him. When stuff like this is happening with Mom, we need to be in contact with each other. He apologized for not responding to me sooner. So now he knows. A silence fell on us like a drenching rain. We were drowning in our own private worries.

The silence snapped when Forrest said that he totally believed every word I was telling him. He even complimented me by saying that my observations were pretty mature for someone my age. I told him that maturity and intellect run in the family. We both had a smile moment, which was much needed. For some dumb reason, all of my emotions were teetering on the edge, ready to shatter like a fallen dish. Pressure was building up in my chest. Tears were filling up in the corners of my eyes. I was determined to keep my cool, because losing it would ruin all the sense of confidence that I had been proudly feeling only an hour earlier.

Leaning over the table, he asked firmly, "Has she seen her doctor?"

I gave him a desperate look. "No, she hasn't."

Forrest grumbled into his hand. "She needs to."

I agreed, but getting her to make the appointment was going to be the tricky part. How in the world am I going to get her to her doctor?

During our entire conversation, Forrest acted more connected, more invested. He truly was listening to me. He truly believed what I was telling him. He even flat-out told me so.

"Summer, it's going to take the both of us to talk Mom into seeing her doctor. I'm not sure what's going on with her, but a trip to the doctor is very much needed."

So we came up with a game plan. Forrest is going to call her first to see if she will talk to him, being that he is older. If Mom agrees to see her doctor after he has talked to her, then he'll text me it's a go. If he has no luck, then I'll be the one to talk to her next.

Again, I feel like I'm ganging up on my mom. You know, the old "two against one" situation. But Forrest explained that we're concerned about her, and we need to show her how our concern will support her in getting help. When he put it that way, it made more sense.

We had to finish up. Mom was going to be home in an hour and a half. I still had some chores to get done so it would look like I had been home the whole time she was at work.

Forrest and I were a bit awkward in saying goodbye. I was so strong until the end. Forrest gave me a half-hug and messed up my hair, telling me that I'll always be his rug-rat little sister. I started to cry. Not a bawling kind of cry, but a steady tears kind of cry. He gave me a harder squeeze and said that he was proud of me, and to call him whenever I needed to talk. Just then, out of nowhere, I asked if that included boy talk. BAM!!! Just like that! I had no control over my words as they lit their way to my brother's ears like a flaming trail of gunpowder. Less than a second after I said it, I wanted to shoot myself. How immature of me! Well, at least this big-time embarrassment got me to stop crying.

Except Forrest cocked his head at me and told me the only way he would listen to me talk about boys is if I would listen to him talk about girls.

I said, "You mean a girl."

And with a boyish smile he said, "Yeah, a certain girl." I lifted my chin high as we walked to his car. We drove back home in quiet, but it was a comfortable kind of quiet. The kind of quiet there is in a movie theater after you see a really good movie.

Metti, I don't know what's wrong with my mom. But if finding help so she can get better brings me closer to my brother, well, I guess all the confusion and scariness can be worth it.

Signed,
Summer, the Proudest Little Sister

October 19

Dear Metti,

Not much to write about. It was a dreary Monday. I had a test in English that I think I pretty much nailed. It's funny: since I started writing to you, my English teacher has told me how improved my writing in class has become. On one page of an essay, she wrote that she thought I had a talent for creative writing. I don't know who to thank: you or me or maybe the both of us. Got homework to do, so bye for now.

Signed,
Summer, wishing her homework would disappear! POOF!!!!!

October 20

Dear Metti,

Today is Tuesday, so Mom and I did our Tuesday thing. You know, I have to say, back when I had this idea for my mom and I to do stuff on Tuesdays, I had no idea that we would stick to the plan. You know, like, we would start off strong, and then it would phase out. Mom would be too busy or too tired, and I'd be too busy or lose interest. Honestly, I really do look forward to Tuesdays. I know my mom does, too, because sometimes I catch her counting the days like kids do waiting for Christmas to come. I'm not sure what we're doing tonight. Mom says she has it planned out, so I'll just have to wait and see.

Oh, yeah, I'm writing this in study hall. Here's something funny: just to show you how mature junior high kids can be. Okay, picture this. My study hall is in the cafeteria, so there are these long, metal tables stretching out across the room. Donald Waroski, a kid I can't stand, is at it again. And what I mean by that is he's drawing attention to himself so everyone will watch him do something stupid. There are two study hall teachers who are supposed to walk around like cops on patrol looking for any bad behavior. Well, today Donald (known as Donny) isn't working alone. He has Jared Pullman go up to one of the teachers, acting like he has this really involved question to ask, buying time for Donny to hit a victim with his "snot ball." You know what a "spit ball" is, right? A snot ball is the same basic concept with one difference. Donny jams a small ball of paper up his nose to get it snotinized to shoot at Laura Mathis, who is today's target.

The first snot ball goes flying with no success. Second ball goes closer, but still misses. Third time's a charm. How gross! It landed in her thick brown hair! Double gross! It is totally stuck in her thick brown hair! Kids are laughing, while Laura is clueless. Donny crams another one up his nose. No, wait, he's cramming one up each nostril. Like, for real?

Nasty: One snot ball came out, but the other one is still jammed up his nostril! He can't blow it out. Gross, now he's frantically picking his nose to get it out. Kids are laughing and making jokes about it. Meanwhile, the teachers are trying to regain order, while Donny is crying because of the pressure of his snot ball.

Oh, more news to report on Laura. She just combed out the snot ball and is freaking out. You need to know that Laura combs her hair like every fifteen seconds. Her hair is her life. Ah, now she's screaming. They just told her it was a snot ball.

This study hall was the bomb of study halls! Off to English class. Wait, Donny has to go to the nurse. The nurse has to get his snot ball out with tweezers. All of this just to get some laughs from people watching him. (I shouldn't talk. . . I rather enjoyed it myself.)

Signing off for now.

October 20 (later)

Dear Metti,

When I got home from school today, my mom was relaxing in our living room. I acted a bit surprised, because she is rarely home before me. I asked her if she was sick or something, and she said, "Yes, but more like no." She told me that we were going to start our Tuesday Time early. I told her that was fine with me.

We went into the kitchen, and there, all set up on our Gateleg table, was a tea party. (More about this table coming later.) It wasn't as childish as it sounds. There were my favorite cookies, arranged just so on a fancy plate with tea cups from the set we played with when I was four years old.

There was also a delicate lace tablecloth that I had never seen before. Mom said that she never got it out when I was younger because it's a very special tablecloth. This tablecloth belonged to my Great-Grandmother Amy, who made it herself as a marriage token to herself. Say what? Back then you had to make your own wedding presents? No, it was more like a symbol of her transforming from a young lady into a married woman. She made it for her kitchen table, which is the Gateleg table. This Gateleg table is pretty cool. It's made of rich, dark walnut. It has these two side panels (actually, they're called "leaves") that fall down alongside the top of the table. So, when you want more space with less table, the leaves fall down. Then, when you want more table with less space, the leaves swing out to each side supported on a "gate" leg, giving the table its name. Pretty cool for an old piece of furniture.

We sat down to our tea and cookies. I was still a bit anxious about all this. Like, I don't know. It's been years since we've had a tea party. It's not what a 13-year-old would have in mind as a fun thing to do. Whatever. It's like nobody's watching us.

Then my mom pulled out a photo album. Of course, it was an album all about yours truly. We giggled and got teary eyed and giggled some more. I didn't laugh as much at myself as I did at the young pictures of Mom, Dad, and Forrest. It was pictures of Forrest that I laughed at the most. He looked like a space alien!

After we were done looking through the album, we ate pizza off of these bone china plates. Mom said, "Oh, if my grandmothers could see me now. They would turn over in their graves. These dishes were reserved for Sunday dinners. I grew up eating Sunday dinners at lunchtime. Sunday dinners were meals like lamb, pork flanks, pot roast, and farm-grown turnips topped with parsley. Fancy meals served on fancy dishes. Men had to wear ties, and women had to wear dresses. Nothing less was acceptable for a Sunday dinner."

I thought to myself: "All this dressing up just because of the dishes? I'm glad I wasn't born during that era."

Without any warning, my mom told me she made an appointment with her family doctor. Forrest had talked to her, but he didn't have to say much to convince her to go.

"I've been rattled, too, by some of the strange stuff I've been doing lately," she told me. She said that sometimes, she just can't connect the thoughts in her "brain space" to the activities in her "life space." Next week, she has an appointment with Dr. Kinley. Dr. Kinley's been our family doctor since Forrest and I were babies. She knows us pretty well. We aren't at the doctor's office much. But there have been a few times I was sure glad she was our doctor.

So, on one hand, I'm glad she has an appointment with her. To me, this means she doesn't have anything very serious. If it were serious, then she would be seeing a specialist right away. On the other hand, if she saw a specialist then whatever is wrong with her could get diagnosed faster. I guess I have to take it one doctor's appointment at a time. Not that I want her to see tons of doctors. I just want her to get better. Back to her old self before all this mental craziness. There are a bazillion medicines out there. I'm sure there's a pill for my mom to take, and she'll perk right back up like nothing was ever wrong. I'm praying for it to be that easy. Waiting until next week is going to feel like FOREVER!!!!!

I almost forgot to tell you that Jason gave me a smile today while we were passing in the halls. I've been in kind of a loopy state, all caught up with my mom. So, things with Jason aren't as drastic for me. I've pretty much forgotten about the football game incident. In fact, I really didn't remember much about it until I saw him. It was a good sign, though, that he smiled at me. I think I smiled back. I don't know.

Metti, if I truly get real with you, I'm scared. What if my mom has a brain tumor or cancer and needs brain surgery? Jason shouldn't be the main thing anymore. It's my mom's health. But I want things to be nice between us. Maybe, when my life has more answers, I can try reconnecting with him. I keep praying and telling myself that it's all good.

Signed,
Summer, who is living one of her longest weeks EVER!

October 21

Dear Metti,

Jason texted me asking if we were good. I slumped down in my chair because I could feel my face getting hot, and I didn't want anyone noticing. I reread his text, which asked me the same question over and over. "Are we good?" Like, what does he mean, "good?" Like, we aren't mad at each other? "Good" in that we are all fine to be friends? Or does "good" mean someday we could be really "good" and get back together?

I slipped up a bit in my chair to sneak a glance at him. I wanted to see if he was watching me. He wasn't watching because he was busy taking notes.

I texted him: "Yeah, it's all good between us. I mean, what are friends for if you can't risk your whole junior high career texting back and forth during class? Why do you ask?"

For the next ten seconds, I froze like I do when I'm anticipating getting a shot. Jason was reading my text.

I read his quick reply: "Summer, you can always make me laugh. And lately I haven't been laughing. I was wondering if you and I could talk sometime. Let me know when you can. Thanks."

At the end of class, I hurried out as soon as the bell started ringing.

Suddenly I was feeling really shy. I know what you're thinking: I should have just texted him back right then and there with a time we could talk. But stupid shy me didn't, so now I have to rethink everything before getting back to him. We have the same lunch period. Maybe that could work out. It sounded like he wanted to really talk, you know, more serious like.

Why am I so anxious? Maybe he wants to talk about what happened at the football game. Well, I kind of didn't give him a chance to explain because at the time I was just so mad. Oh, I sure hope that's not what he wants to talk about. You know how much of a jerk I was that night. Do I ever have a headache! Got to go to sleep. I think that my head is going to pound right through my pillow, it hurts so bad.

Signed,
Summer, whose head feels like
it's going to EXPLODE!

October 22

Dear Metti,

Well, I did get a good night's sleep last night. It helps to go to bed earlier, especially when you have the headache of the century. There are these girls in my gym class who are always trying to get out of class by saying they have a migraine. (Or it's because they have their periods.) Usually these girls are so dramatic about it. Oh, and they talk about how they don't want to get out of bed when they have their periods. They act so pathetic.

Jason saw me in the halls today and gave me a little wave. I gave him a wave back. He looked a bit rough with his hair messed up. His hair is never messed up. He's really serious about his hair. He styles it, gels it, then sprays it. His hair wouldn't move in a hurricane.

All of this weirdness is a bit too much. I'm anxious about my mom's doctor's appointment. I'm anxious about talking with Jason. How am I going to handle it all?

Metti, you sure are lucky to be a journal. What could you possibly be anxious about?

Signed,
Summer, who wishes she had a
genie to grant her THREE wishes!

Summer's Three Wishes

1.) To take away whatever is wrong with my mom

2.) For Jason to like me again. All right, for Jason and I to confide in each other as friends.

3.) For Jason to like me again. (If a genie can grant you three wishes, it certainly will know when your wishes are lies. So, I might as well be honest about them.)

October 24

Dear Metti,

Drowning in homework, so I don't have time to write.

Signed,
Summer, who would love to
get paid for doing homework

October 26

Dear Metti,

Just two more days to go, and Mom will go to see the doctor. I can hardly wait. Yesterday, Mom was rushing around the house, wondering where she'd put the checkbook. Thirty minutes must have gone by, and she still didn't know where the checkbook had gone.

Then I heard a yelp coming from the kitchen. I slid on my socks as I rounded the corner to find my mom stretched out, lying on her stomach, warning me about the black hole in the kitchen floor. She cautiously waved at me not to come any closer for fear I'd fall in the hole.

I matter-of-factly told her there wasn't a hole of any kind in our kitchen floor. "Mom, what the heck are you talking about? The floor is solid. Are you joking with me?"

But she was for real. She was so bent on the fact that there actually was a black hole in the kitchen floor. She was totally convinced that this is where the checkbook must be. Then she started to carry on about how every home has a "black hole" in it. It's in these black holes that you find the missing sock matches, keys to old locks, loose change, and yes, the checkbook! No matter what I said to her, she was totally convinced that there was a hole in the floor with the checkbook somewhere hidden in it.

"Mom, the floor is solid. There is nothing wrong with it. Look, I can walk on it."

Just as I was about to step out and walk across the floor to her, she screamed out at me! "Summer, don't you move another inch, or you'll fall in!" I paused, wondering what I should do, but she kept yelling. "Please, Summer, stop scaring me! You're going to fall in this horrible hole."

"Scare you? What the heck are you doing to me? Mom, you're totally freaking me out! If this is a joke, you have gone too far. Do you hear me? Not funny! I repeat: there is no hole in the floor!"

Silence dropped in the room like an anchor dropped from its ship. My hands were sweating. My heart was pounding out through my ears. I felt so anxious, so nervous, so out of control with what was happening to my mom. What we were experiencing in the kitchen of our very own home. I fixed my eyes on my mother. She no longer was acting in fear of my safety, but now was reacting to this most bizarre situation.

"Summer, honey, I wasn't joking with you. I was certain I saw what I saw. A black hole in the floor right here," she said in a raspy voice.

"Mom, do you see a hole now?"

She raised herself up like a fallen tree and whispered, "No."

"Mom, what's going on with you?" I asked her. I think I was in a mild state of shock.

"Summer, sweetie, I really don't know. What I do know is that I need help. I totally know that. As for what's wrong with me, I have no idea." Then she walked over to me, going straight through what had been the "black hole."

My mother hid her face in her hands. We instinctively reached out for one another, grabbed hold of each other, and cried.

No: we sobbed. My mom tries so hard to be strong for me, for herself, for the both of us. But her life has gone so wacko! So it has to be me now who is strong for her, for me, for the both of us.

Mom went to bed before I did. I immediately had to call Forrest and fill him in on this bizarre incident with Mom. This was not a texting type of thing. I needed to talk to him! I called him around 10:15 hoping it was late enough for him not to be studying. Thank goodness, he answered when I called.

"Forrest, Mom is out of her mind, and I don't know what to do about it! I'm serious, Forrest she's out of her mind. You wouldn't believe what she did tonight." I was talking so fast, yet I felt like my words were coming out of my mouth like toothpaste at the end of the tube, all slow and sticky.

"Summer, calm down and take a breath. What are you talking about? Is Mom hurt? Did something happen that you both got hurt? What's going on?" I heard some alarm in Forrest's voice as he shot out question after question.

"Mom thought, I mean really thought, there was a black hole in the kitchen floor. In our very own, in our house, kitchen floor!" I exhaled so much it sounded like a wind tunnel.

"What?" More alarm in his voice.

"A black hole in our kitchen floor. I was in the living room when I heard her yelp and I ran to the kitchen to see if she was okay. And there she was, sprawled out on the floor, afraid that she and I would fall into the black hole." My voice was shaking, my teeth were chattering, and my body felt all tied up like a mummy. Hearing myself as these words come out of my mouth made the whole experience even more difficult to believe, much less understand.

Forrest was agitated. He released a lot of apprehension by whispering things under his breath. I couldn't really hear him. Nor do I think he wanted for me to hear him.

"Summer, do you know what a hallucination is?"

"Yeah, when you think you see something that really isn't there to be seen. Mom was hallucinating a black hole in our kitchen floor." This was the only tiniest part that made any kind of sense.

"Well, sometimes people will be so stressed out that they begin to hallucinate. Maybe this is the case for Mom. You know, she might be so stressed out about how she can't remember things that she is hallucinating to release the intense stress bottled up inside. Oh, maybe she had an adverse side effect to a medication? Summer, there could be some simple explanations to it." My intellectual oversized brain-celled brother thinks that Mom is fearing for our lives from an imaginary black hole in our kitchen because of STRESS! I'm pretty stressed out, and am I hallucinating?

I'm glad I called him, I guess; I don't know. I'm not feeling much better about it. Maybe Forrest was protecting me from something he thinks is more serious with Mom? Maybe he's telling it like it is? Maybe he's going to be right on all counts. But I'm not buying the stressed-out theory. No, not one bit.

Metti, I'm so glad I have you to confide in and not just Forrest. That brother is driving me crazy almost as much as Mom. I have to keep myself in balance. Take one thing at a time. Just one thing at a time.

Signed,
Summer, who should be
the stressed out one!

October 27

Dear Metti,

I can't believe a week has gone by since our last Tuesday Time. At first, the week was going really slow. Then it picked up and has flown by me. I guess this is a good thing, since I thought I'd be waiting forever until Mom's doctor's appointment. Here it is, only a day away. I'm so glad we have plans for tonight. This way, both Mom and I are preoccupied, so tomorrow will come all the faster.

For our Tuesday Time, we are going to the movies. It's going to sound lame, but the movie is a cartoon. Kids have been talking about it in school without anybody giving them a hard time. The movie is about this mouse who, all her life, believes that she is a mouse. Well, that makes sense, because she is a mouse. Then, one day, the mouse sneaks into the castle of very big (and rich) humans, only to overhear that the king and queen's daughter had a spell cast on her—which, you guessed, it changed her into a mouse. It's set in the cartoon movie world, so you know, animals can talk, eat at a table with manners, and understand singing humans. The movie is called Lady Acorpian. The story takes place in the magical land of Acorpian. I'll let you know if it's good or not. Buttered popcorn, here I come!

Signed,
Summer, who still loves a good fairytale

October 28

Dear Metti,

The day has finally arrived. My mom went to the doctor's today. She said that overall, it went well. She doesn't have high blood pressure or high cholesterol. Her heart rate was up, but that's because she was nervous.

I'm so proud of her. You see, my mom isn't one to draw attention to herself. When in conversation with other people, she talks very little about herself. Even when it means telling the doctor what's going on with her, she still doesn't say much. But today, during her appointment, she told the doctor everything. She even cried at points.

The bottom line is this: the family doctor wants her to see a specialist who knows more about her symptoms. This specialist will do tests that check the memory part of her brain. I forget what the specialist is called. (Maybe I should go with her, since I can't remember what the doctor is called that helps people with their memory. So ironic!) Luckily, Mom wrote the specialist's name down, and she has an appointment for two weeks from now.

I asked Mom if she felt better after talking to our doctor. She said that she was pretty tired and just wanted to go to bed. I was so itching to ask her about medicine that could help her get better. Or diet plans that help your body build up resistance naturally. But I bit my tongue. She did look pretty exhausted. It's not too often that my mom goes to bed before me. Tonight was an all-out record: At 7:30, her bedroom lights were out. She'll be more like Mom again in the morning.

Oh, by the way, the movie from last night, Lady Acorpian, wasn't too bad. In fact, it was pretty good. The mouse was totally cute. So now I want a pet mouse to keep in my room. (My mom yelped when I told her that. Can't knock a girl for trying.) It was your typical fairytale kind of story. But it was a more sophisticated type of fairytale. It was nice just to escape into another world even if it was in fairytale land. For my token to put in Mom's book: a nicely colored picture of a very, very cute mouse.

Signed,
Summer, who wants a cute pet mouse

October 29

Dear Metti,

Today I asked my mom for the name of the specialist she's going to see. She said that her specialist's name is Dr. Rebecca Robinson. That isn't what I wanted to know, exactly. What I want to know is what kind of specialist she is. Like an orthodontist is a specialized kind of dentist for fixing teeth with braces. I don't know why this is important to me. It just is. I asked her about it again, and she snapped at me, so I stopped asking.

Yeah, we both are short on patience. We wanted to know more information, and more isn't here yet. We wanted to have more answers, and they aren't here yet. Mom can snap at me. I'd be a lot worse with people if I was her. Shoot, she's the one all of this unknown stuff is directly affecting.

Forrest called to check with Mom about her appointment. She told him same as she told me. I'm glad he called her. I texted Forrest when I knew they were done talking. I asked him if he knew the name of the kind of specialist who deals with memory testing. He said he didn't know but would do a Google search for me.

"Really?"

"Yeah, really, I'm a college student. I can do a little internet search."

Whatever floats your boat, Forrest. Go for it. That's just the way he is, my big brother. Give him a homework assignment that requires research, and he's all over it like a dog to his bone. I could probably have Googled it right there, but no. Forrest will figure it out.

I was going to ask about how things were going on the "girlfriend front." I chose not to ask simply because I was so sleepy, I caught myself nodding off during our conversation.

Signed,
Summer the Sleepy

October 30

Dear Metti,

After supper tonight, Mom and I made our plans for Halloween. She wasn't sure I would still want to participate. It has become a tradition of sorts, I walk in the Halloween parade while mom drives the bookmobile. I told her I was all in again this year. I asked her the theme, and she said it's "Wild About Reading." Well, this year's theme is lots easier than other year's themes. Last year's theme was "Reading Is Out of This World." I had to dress up like an oversized ball of aluminum foil. I was going for the "space creature" look. Then one year, I was Emily Elizabeth while a coworker of Mom's was Clifford the Big Red Dog. My favorite Halloween theme was "Reading Is Magical." That year I dressed up like an elegant princess. So for this year, I will dress up like a cheetah. I have a cheetah fleece vest, black leggings, cheetah gloves, a black long-sleeved shirt, cheetah ears, and a tail. I'll paint my face with a cheetah design and wear my cheetah print boots. Yep, I still get excited for Halloween!

Signed,
Summer, who came up with
the purrrfect wild cat costume

October 31

Dear Metti,

Tonight was so much fun! But do my legs ache from all the walking. Mom was a pro at driving the bookmobile. Mom is a backup driver for the library's bookmobile. She has her CDL (Certified Driver's License) and everything, making her legal to drive. The regular driver, Cindy, has younger children, so Mom usually drives in the parade so Cindy can enjoy watching with her family.

Mom said that my makeup came out really good. I guess so, because lots of children asked me to roar when I handed them their bookmarks. (Libraries don't believe in handing out candy. Not even just one time out of the year.) I liked the attention, you know. As people were watching the parade, they were watching me too. I felt like I was part of a show. Anyway, the parade was good. More groups this year participated than last year. We didn't win a prize, but I had fun.

Signed,
Summer, who is all ready to
plan for next year!

November 1

Dear Metti,

I'm feeling overwhelmed with writing to you. Don't get me wrong. I love writing. I never in my wildest dreams thought that I would be a journal writer. In fact, the word "writer" gives me the tingles. You know, the kind of tingles you get on a rollercoaster ride. The thrill, the anticipation, the daringness, the RIDE!!!

This is how I feel when I'm writing to you. It thrills me because I have something so totally my own. I anticipate writing to you because I usually have a lot to say. It's daring because I share the very core of my soul with you, and only with you. The RIDE!

Sometimes I don't write to you. Instead, I read over stuff I have already written. As I read, I see it like a ride of words and emotions that go up and down depending on what's going on in my life.

But lately, I've been feeling overwhelmed with writing. I feel as though I have to keep you informed about everything in my life. I simply can't do that. Telling you about my friends, school, Mom, the "whatever" relationship Jason and I have, Forrest— and I hardly ever tell you stuff about my dad. It just seems like too much for me to write about every single time something does or doesn't happen with all this in my life.

So, could we say that I'll write about stuff that's happening in my life that I want and need to write about? I guess I pretty much have been doing that so far. I mean, I still have friends, and I still do stuff with my friends, but I don't write about it much because I'm good with it that way.

What I really have to write about is the stuff that's in me. I don't do much thinking when I'm writing. I just let it flow. The words and thoughts come as they please. At times, I feel like a storyteller or an author. Like the time I told you all about my Great-Grandma Roxie. It just came out. In my mind, I saw pictures of my great-grandma in her restaurant with lit lamps on the walls and tables full of hungry customers. It's weird. Once I get a picture or image in my head, I have to write about it to get it out of my head.

So, are we good? I never really thought about it until now. I write from my heart first and from my head second. I don't know if this is a good thing or not. . . I mean, I never thought much about the right way to write in a journal. I want to keep on writing so you can keep on being Metti.

Signed,
Summer the Journalist

P.S. *I have to buy another notebook soon. It has to be special. Not just any notebook will do.*

November 3

Dear Metti,

Today is Tuesday, and I'm not sure what's going on. I don't know why, but I'm in a really mellow mood. Nothing went wrong, but nothing went right either. I just don't feel like myself today. It doesn't help that it's a chilly, windy day. I don't even know if I said two words to anyone in school. I remember throwing my sneakers into my gym locker because the laces broke off, so I had to borrow a pair from the gym teacher, who gave me a check for not being completely prepared for class. Say what? Like I can control when my laces are going to break. Oh, I should have an extra pair in my locker for when things like this happen. REALLY? I guess as part of our Tuesday Time, I'll be buying shoelaces. This works because I have to get another notebook for my journaling. I think I'm going to take a nap while I wait for my mom to come home. Just need to do some mellowing out. Until later.

November 3 (later)

Dear Metti,

Well, my "mellowing out" nap sure helped. That's the good thing. But will I sleep tonight? We had grilled cheese sandwiches with tomato soup for supper. You may be wondering why I'm telling you about silly grilled cheese and tomato soup. Because we don't eat these two foods like most people do. We cut up the grilled cheese sandwich into small squares or chunks and put them into the soup. On top of that we sprinkle in oregano. Delicious! Just another family weirdness we have.

I told Mom about the gym class drama. She wasn't upset about me getting the check. She agreed that a trip to the drug store would be a good idea. I just casually mentioned that I needed a notebook for my journaling. She looked at me and thought I was taking a journaling class in school. I told her it was for my journaling at home. It totally never, ever dawned on me that I should have told my mom how I journal in the diary she gave me on my 13th birthday.

She looked stunned. "Summer, you do what? You actually started keeping a diary in the notebook I gave you?"

My face blushed so bad. When she realized that I needed another notebook so I could keep journaling, she just about fainted. Then she said something to me that I thought was kind of profound.

"The relationship between a writer and her words can become so privately known to the world. Choose a notebook that reflects your world of words."

You know, I can so relate to Anne Frank more and more. Well, not the going into hiding to save my life stuff, but the writing part. She wrote down countless thoughts and ideas. She shared feelings that went so deep. She had dreams like any 13-year-old girl. But none of her written world came true for her. At the time Anne Frank was pouring herself out through her journal, it was all very private. Just Anne and her journal Kitty. But then her private world of words publicly exploded the moment her dairy got published. Anne Frank's diary has been translated into bazillion different languages, made into plays, and even developed into a movie. So this is what my mom means when she says authors of journals and diaries become "privately known to the world." It's so sad she isn't alive to see how her diary, Kitty, opened the eyes of so many important people. Kitty became the ghost voice of Anne.

As for me, let's get this straight, right here and now. There is no way my journal is going to be read by anyone out there in the real world. No translations, no plays, no movies. Being a journal author is a very private thing. I intend to keep it that way! (Nope, not for a million dollars would I share my journal.)

Signed,
Private Summer (get it?)

P.S. *My new journal is beautiful. It has a satin look to it, and the cover has a graceful white bird and Chinese characters going down the left side. It's the same look as my mom's memory book. The really cool part about my new journal is what the characters mean: "Write on the wings of your dreams." Metti, it's going to take some getting used to having two of you.*

November 6

Dear Metti,

Wow! I feel like a new person. I've been out of it for the past couple days. My headache turned into a bad sinus infection. And my chills turned into a fever. It was bad enough that my mom stayed home with me for a day. All I really did was sleep and sleep some more. I would wake up to go to the bathroom and then right back to bed to sleep.

Good news: I'm feeling much better. Bad news: I missed two days of school. I hate catching up on schoolwork.

Oh, by the way, Forrest called to see how I was feeling. He was calling Mom about something, and then he wanted to talk to me. He did find out some info about the specialist Mom is going to see. I totally forgot about that while I was sick, or I would have just Googled it myself! I don't need to be a college kid to work my cell phone, but I think it made Forrest feel like he was helping.

It turns out that there are three kinds of memory specialists. One is a neurologist, who specializes in diseases the brain and nervous system can get. Then there is a psychiatrist, who specializes in what affects your mood and the workings of your mind. Lastly, there is a neuropsychologist, who has training in testing your memory and other stuff you do mentally. So on the 10th, my mom is seeing a Dr. Rebecca Robinson, who is a neuropsychologist. Mom said she'll be doing some memory tests. Sounds pretty painless to me. I'm still not sure what this all means, but at least we are getting closer to the appointment. Maybe then, we'll all understand better.

Signed,
Summer, in waiting

November 7

Dear Metti,

Mom had a crazy moment again. The phone was ringing just as I came into the house after school. Mom was at work. When I answered the phone, it was our neighbor Mrs. Wagner. She lives across the street and two houses down. She made small talk at first, you know, how are you doing in school, what grade are you in now, and oh, how you're growing up so fast, I bet your mother is proud of you.

I started to tune her out until she said, "Speaking of your mother, is she feeling alright?"

I answered, "Yes, she's feeling fine." Lying between my teeth. In my head I was screaming, "No she's not fine! Not really! Not at all! She forgets simple things. She gets lost on the way home from places she's been to a thousand times. And she thinks there's a black hole in our kitchen floor."

Instead, I took some deep breaths and calmly said, "Why do you ask?"

"Well, I'm asking because the other day she was going to your mailbox as I was sweeping my sidewalk. Your mother and I—in fact your whole family and I—have known each other for over ten years. We have never had any neighborly problems. Well, I started to chit-chat with your mother, and she looked at me as if I had two heads. No, it was worse than that. Your mother looked at me as if she had never seen me before. I asked her how she was doing. And, plain as day, she responded very strangely.

She said, 'Excuse, me, do I know you? I mean, have we ever met before?' I stared back at her, wondering what to say. Then she told me that I must be a new neighbor in the neighborhood. Summer, is everything alright with your mother?"

I felt like a prize fighter. Inside, I was punching away all this craziness that Mrs. Wagner was telling me about Mom. Every time she said something that I didn't want to hear I would punch it away. But then it all became too much and I felt like the wind got punched out of me.

"Mrs. Wagner, my mom hasn't been feeling herself lately. It's nothing too serious. Just that she's out of sorts. She's been to the doctors, and they are working on getting her better. Thank you for your concern. And my mom didn't mean anything by not knowing who you are. She'll know that you are still our neighbor."

Then this very old, very cold, very strange word came out of Mrs. Wagner's mouth. She told me how her late husband Charlie used to be that way toward people when he was having a bad day with his Alzheimer's. What the heck is Alzheimer's? It certainly sounded German or Greek, or something not American.

I was finally able to say goodbye. After I hung up, my hands were shaking. I couldn't believe Mom had no idea who our very dear Mrs. Wagner was!

I know what you're thinking, Metti, I could Google this mysterious Alzheimer's thing that sounds like the name of Frankenstein's cousin. But I'm not going to do that. I'm not going to stress myself out any more than I already am. I'm going to wait for the diagnosis from the doctors. I'm going to wait until whatever is wrong with my mom is confirmed by her doctor. Then, and only then will I do any kind of research. Mom isn't turning into a monster. She just has some brain issues right now—that's all. She'll get better. The doctors will know how to fix it. I'm sure of it!

November 10th just can't come soon enough. I'm sure my mom doesn't have Alzheimer's, now that I think of it. Mr. Wagner was an old man when he died. My mom is only 55. (Yeah, that's old to me, but you know what I mean.)

Signed,
Summer, the daughter who feels
like she's the mom to her mom

November 7 (later)

Dear Metti,

I tried calling Forrest around 7:30 tonight, but he didn't answer, so I texted him to call me. I sure hope he calls me back and soon. I feel so weird. Now the neighbors are getting into whatever is wrong with my mom. I trust Mrs. Wagner. I mean, we have been neighbors like for forever. I know she isn't going to be talking about Mom to other neighbors. Mrs. Wagner isn't that type of neighbor. You know, gossiping about one neighbor's business to another. And she did mention that her husband had some health issues, so she should certainly understand how helpful it is to keep private things private.

I hear my phone ringing. I hope it's Forrest—

No such luck. It was a telemarketer.

I hate waiting. Oh, my gosh, I really need to talk to my brother!

Signed,

Summer, who needs to talk to Forrest

November 8

Dear Metti,

I fell asleep last night before Forrest called me back, but he did call me back. Now I have to find time today to talk to him without Mom noticing.

This is getting too stressful. It's not that Mom doesn't want me and Forrest to talk. It's just that she wants to know what we're talking about. I think she's getting nervous about us ganging up on her. Or maybe that's just how I think she sees it because that's how I'm feeling.

Oh, Metti, what can I do? I don't want my mom to feel like she's being spied on or something. But I have to keep Forrest in the loop. Two more days, and I'll have answers, my mom will have answers—wonderful, glorious answers so she can get better. Two more days to go!

Signed,
Summer, who just can't WAIT!!!!!!!!!

November 9

Dear Metti,

I finally got a chance to talk to Forrest.

I told him about the whole Mom and Mrs. Wagner incident. He didn't say much until I mentioned how Mrs. Wagner said something about Alzheimer's. Then his silence invaded me like a metallic fog.

"Forrest, are you listening to me? What does this Alzheimer's Mrs. Wagner told me about have to do with Mom? Do you know anything about it?"

"I know a little bit about it. Alzheimer's is a disease that old people get. Yeah, it has to do with the brain or memory or something like that. But it's an old person's disease. Mom isn't even close to being old. So don't worry about it being Alzheimer's. Case in point: Charlie Wagner was old when he died."

He sounded so matter-of-fact about it all. What the heck was I worrying about? Mom is only 55 years old. She couldn't possibly have an old person's sickness. Forrest still has no idea what's going on with Mom. We all will be so relieved after we get some answers from the doctors. Just twenty-four hours left for that to happen.

Signed,
Summer, who hopes time flies because
I am not having fun waiting!

November 10

Dear Metti,

I had a hard time focusing in school today. Mom took the day off from work for her appointment. When I got home, she was lying on the couch, spaced-out, looking up at the ceiling fan. I walked in, hoping she would hear me and start telling me about her appointment. She heard me, but instead of telling me about her appointment, she started to talk about the ceiling fan.

"Summer, this ceiling fan and I have so much in common. My life is just spinning around and around with only one direction to go—around. Sometimes I can function in life going at a fast speed. Other times, I'm totally on slow, barely moving. It's rare that I'm on medium speed. You know, right in the middle, where I feel in control of my life. Then there are days like today, when I'm just stopped. I have no movement whatsoever. Just like this fan is right now. Stopped."

"That's—that's weird, Mom." I mean, what else could I say?

Finally, she sat up to talk more. She really didn't have any filters on the conversation, which was good and bad. She told me she'd had two different types of brain tests done. The first test was a CT scan. She explained that a CT scan is like an x-ray of the brain. The scan shows the supply of brain cells in the temporal lobe. Part of this area has the hippocampus. Mom called it the "hippo," and it helps with a person's memory functions. I kept thinking to myself, "So, this means exactly what?" I wanted Mom to get to the point already.

Then she said it: "The memory area of my 'hippo' shows a decrease in brain cells. This means that I have a memory-related disease. So, the doctors want to take more tests, like an MRI of my brain. The next doctor to see is a neurologist."

I told her that she was going to be okay. I shared with her how medicine could help her, or maybe it would have to be a treatment of some kind. But I told her that she's going to be fine. This all makes sense to me, because now, the doctors know what's wrong—so they can fix it.

But Mom isn't so sure it will be that easy. She described to me how she totally failed the second test she took. It was just her and the doctor in a comfortable, quiet room. The doctor would ask her questions, and then she would answer them. This was fine, until the doctor asked her to repeat the answers only a minute later. Mom said it got harder because she had to remember things in certain order, like numbers, names, and addresses. She said that everything the doctor told her just flowed out, seeping away from any chance of remembering.

"I failed miserably, Summer. It's like my brain has holes in it."

In about two weeks, Mom has to go back and get an MRI test done. It's the same idea of taking pictures of her brain, but this test will show more details.

Then she told me something I wasn't prepared for, not in a million years. She told me that the doctors are aware of what has been going on at home with my mom's forgetfulness and strange behavior. I don't know why this freaked me out, but it did. I thought that whatever weird stuff my mom was doing at home was our secret. You know, the private home stuff that you don't share with anyone, not even your best friend. But now it's out there. It seems to be okay with my mom, but not with me, not at ALL! She could be put in a hospital for wackos.

Finally, I convinced myself that it would all be okay. Whatever is going on medically is fine for the doctors to know. It's their job to know so they can find a way of fixing it.

Then, Mom slammed me again. She said I should go with her to her next appointment. SAY WHAT!!!? The doctors feel that it's very important for someone who lives with Mom and knows her fairly well to come with her to the appointments. This is helpful because I can tell the doctors what's going on with Mom without stressing her out by asking her to remember what's important to tell them.

I told her I'd think about it. But in my mind, I was screaming, "No way—not on your life!"

I asked Mom if she was okay. She said yes and no. Sometimes not knowing is just as scary as knowing. I agreed with her.

Signed,
Summer in the Twilight Zone

November 13

Dear Metti,

Call my mom CRAZY!!!! This time it isn't that kind of crazy. We both got so wrapped up in Mom's doctor's appointment on the 10th that we forgot it was a Tuesday for us to do our Tuesday Time. SOOOOOOO. . . My mom says we need to make up for it today, which happens to be Friday the 13th!!!!!!!!

She told me to go change my clothes so I was wearing as much black as possible. We got into the car. Our first stop was at the grocery store, where we bought 13 double-chocolate chocolate chip cookies. Then we stopped at the pet store to look at the black cats. (We are not adopting a cat of any color. I do not like cats!) Next, we went to a fast food restaurant to buy french fries. This was my crazy mom; she threw salt over her shoulder before salting her fries.

As we walked up the sidewalk to our front door, we skipped over the cracks. Lastly, we streamed a scary movie. I don't know which was scarier: the way my mom got so into celebrating Friday the 13th, or the movie we saw about campers mysteriously disappearing in the woods. I told my mom that she just ruined any chance of me being a summer camp counselor.

We didn't watch the whole thing. We both are wimps when it comes to scary movies. Until the next Friday the 13th!

Signed,
Summer the Ghost Slayer (NOT)

November 15

Dear Metti,

The strangest thing happened today, and it had nothing to do with my mom. I'm still so in shock that I don't know if I'll be able to write about it. No, it had nothing to do with Forrest or any of my friends or even Jason.

It had all to do with my dad. I haven't written about him in like forever because, well, he isn't in my life that much. He was in Brazil on business for two months. So, you can imagine how surprised I was when he showed up on our front porch, asking if we wanted to go out for a hamburger or something. Yes, me and my mom! My dad doesn't even eat hamburgers!

I stared at my mom, and my mom stared back at me. We both stood there like deer in the headlights. After some small talk, Mom said, "Sure. Why not? Especially if you're paying, Todd."

So out the door we went, like old times, and I was about to vomit from the ball of nerves taking over my stomach. We all went in Dad's car to Daisy's Burger Place. The slogan on her sign reads, "We grill to thrill." Yeah, no thrill is in the air tonight—try more like chill.

It was totally weird having the three of us sitting at the same table, talking to each other like we were pulling buckets of words out of a deep dry well. Then crash! A flood came in just four words, just one stupid sentence out of the mouth of my stupid father.

He announced to us like we were at one of his business

meetings: "I'm moving to California."

What the heck! My mom just looked up at the ceiling for like a minute to get her composure.

I spared Dad nothing. I yelled at him. That's when the slippery secretive snake jumped out of my mouth. "You're leaving when Mom's sick. How dare you? It's always about you! Just for once, could you force yourself to think of her?"

My mom's eyes grew to the size of fried eggs. My dad was actually quiet for all of three seconds.

Then the "old times" started. Dad questioned Mom about her health, Mom blamed Dad for not being involved, because if he had been just a little bit involved, he would know about these things. Back and forth it went, so I left the table.

I walked around to the back of the building, wanting my personal space. I sat down at a picnic table, ready to pound my fists on its decaying boards. Then there, in the middle of my rage, who should show up? My selfish father! He sat down next to me and told me that Forrest gave him a hint about Mom's health and seeing the doctors.

Then came the whopper of a line: "Summer, this job in California is a once-in-a-lifetime job."

Blah, blah, blah, blah. I put my hand up and told him to stop talking about whatever dream job it is. I didn't want to hear about it. I just wanted to go home.

Mom said that Dad will be moving the first of the year. She also mentioned that I should work things out with him before he leaves. Fat chance of that ever happening. Fat chance.

I don't know if I should be mad at Forrest or not. I mean, just when we were starting to get along, he has to spill the beans to Dad.

But then, maybe deep inside, I wanted Dad to know about Mom so he might come back and fall in love with her again as he takes care of her. Fat chance of that ever happening either. Fat chance!

Life just seems to be filled with a lot of fat chances. Well, count one out. I told Mom I would go to her doctor's appointments with her. Yeah, it hit me after seeing what my dad was doing: I thought maybe I was doing a bit of the same. If going to Mom's doctor's appointments can help her, then that's what I have to push myself to do. Unlike my dad, who moves to California. Yep, he's a runner. He's running from Mom, me, and even Forrest. Go ahead, Dad. Run to California. See if I care.

Signed,
Summer, who HATES CALIFORNIA

November 16

Dear Metti,

It's been a while, like forever, since I have written about school. I can't believe that it was just this past summer I was so into Jason, wanting to be together again. That seems like ninety years ago. To tell you the truth, I haven't thought of him for a long time. I don't see him in school much, either. And when I do, he's talking to his squad of friends that doesn't include me.

Friends are at a distance for me. I'm not a total loner, but close to it. I have people I can talk to in the halls at school, but it pretty much stops there. I feel like I've grown up past everyone else, yet at the same time, I feel so behind. I feel like I'm living in a bubble.

As far as my relationship with my dad, I'll make an effort to make some peace between us. Life can be so crazy and confusing and downright maddening.

My mom's next appointment is on November 24th. I don't even know what to think about that. I just want to have some control in my life.

Signed,
Summer, whose life is so aimless

November 17

Dear Metti,

Today is Tuesday. My mom said that I could be in charge of our activity. I don't know what to do. I'm writing to you instead of paying attention to the history teacher. For all he knows, I'm taking notes.

Hey, I just had a brainstorm about what to do for our Tuesday Time. It's going to sound totally weird and all, but I think we're going to Linburg Park. When I was little, I went there every day of my life because I loved the swings. Today, I feel like swinging on the swings. There's something about swinging and clearing your mind. I totally need to clear my mind. See you later tonight.

November 17 (later)

Dear Metti,

Well, Mom and I did go to the park. We were really crazy and packed a picnic dinner. So there we were, sitting under a pavilion, dressed in our warmest clothes, having a picnic. We drank hot chocolate with our gooey chocolate chip cookies. Then we swung on the swings. All was going great until my mom yelled, "Summer, I have to stop! I'm going to throw up!" So she stopped, but I kept on swinging. I could have been there all night, just swinging.

Signed,
Summer the Swinger! (get it?)

November 19

Dear Metti,

Today my mom was off. She kept complaining about a hole in the bathroom ceiling. I told her there wasn't any hole. She insisted that there was one because the window (that's in the bathroom) was dirty. Maybe I should agree with her. Yeah, I want a hole in the bathroom ceiling. A hole big enough for me to float up through and get away for a while.

Signed,
Summer the Ceiling Escape Artist

November 20

Dear Metti,

Excuse me in advance for being really mad. Both Mom and Dad said that I had to go to my dad's this weekend to help sort out some stuff of mine that I keep at his apartment. Like, I don't have much at my dad's. I'm not there very often. Hasn't he noticed that by now? As for working out the other stuff, you can count me out. I'm not talking to him. He made his decision, so he has to live with it, not ME!

Signed,
Summer, who is too mad for words

November 21

Dear Metti,

I'm at my dad's apartment. Forrest has been in and out, but mostly out because of his upcoming finals. I didn't know this, but I guess it has become serious between Forrest and his girlfriend, Clara Rose. Typical of my brother to tell us he has a girlfriend, but forget to keep us up-to-date afterward.

My dad is going through stuff in his kitchen. He asked me if I would help. No, not going to do it. So I came in my "guest" room to write to you. I hope he breaks some glasses. That's how it feels inside, like a shattered mirror. Nothing seems real anymore, and it's breaking up all around me.

Signed,
Summer, who really wants to cry

November 22

Dear Metti,

Still at Dad's, just going through the motions. I'll be home at suppertime. Hope I can hang in there that long.

Signed,
Summer the Robot

November 23

Dear Metti,

I made it home. Not in the mood for writing. Sorry.

Signed,
Summer, who has shut down

November 24

Dear Metti,

Can my life get any WORSE?!!!!!!!!!!!! Mom had her doctor's appointment, and the results came back from her test. Her MRI showed that she has a 25% loss of brain cells in a certain section of her brain.

My mom knows what's wrong with her. And it's bad news. It isn't cancer or a giant flesh-eating tumor. It's called early-onset Alzheimer's disease. It's just like what Mrs. Wagner said it could be like with her husband Charlie. But he was old. I asked her about medicines she can take or surgeries she could have done, or treatments, or anything that would help her get better. She said there are some medicines, but they're still in the experimental stage. Vitamins are important, along with a regular routine and exercise.

I told her I didn't get it. I demanded she tell me what's wrong. Where is she sick? I was freaking out!

"It's my brain," she said very calmly. "My brain is sick. My brain is sick, and there isn't a cure for it to get better."

We cried on the kitchen floor like a couple of wailing babies. This is how we spent our Tuesday Time together.

Signed,
Summer, who is losing everything

November 26

Dear Metti,

Today is Thanksgiving. I ate a bowl of mashed potatoes. Forrest is home for the holiday. Mom told him her bad news. He cried. First time ever I've seen my brother cry.

Signed,
Summer, who is thankful for what?

November 27

Dear Metti,

Forrest and I talked today while Mom took a very long nap. Being the day after Thanksgiving, the library was closed. Thank goodness Mom didn't have to go to work.

Forrest asked me if I was okay. Like, my brother is so intellectually smart, yet he asks the stupidest questions.

I yelled in his face, "NO, I'M NOT OKAY!" I think a drop of spit landed on his perfect nose!

We went silent for a while. Then he apologized for asking such a stupid question. I asked him what we were going to do. He gave me an answer I never thought would come out of his mouth.

"Summer, we are in this together because our family is getting smaller—like down to the two of us. With Mom sick and Dad moving to California, we don't have much choice but to stick together. I had the doctor's office call me before Mom told me. So I've known about her Alzheimer's. I've been doing some research. Summer, it isn't good for Mom, but it isn't necessarily horrible for her either. Early-onset Alzheimer's disease can progress slowly or quickly; it all depends on the nature of the beast. Clara Rose's aunt had Alzheimer's, so she knows stuff about it. Her aunt died when she was in her mid-eighties. Mom is a fighter, and so are we."

I wrapped my arms around Forrest's shoulders like they were a life ring. I held onto him so tightly, fearing that I would drown in a wave of grief. I'm being emotionally shipwrecked by a storm named "Alzheimer's." I could taste the saltiness of my tears as I cried.

Signed,
Summer, who is lost at sea

November 28

Dear Metti,

I don't feel much like writing. I hope you understand.

Signed,
Summer, who just wants to sleep

November 29

Dear Metti,

I don't want to write anymore. Do you understand? I don't want to write to you anymore. I have nothing to share. I have nothing to write about. Do you understand? Please say you do. Tuesday is in two days. What are Mom and I going to do for our Tuesday Time together? She's different now. It won't be the same. I can't do it. I won't do it. I wish there were never any more Tuesdays to be lived. That's it. I'm done.

Signed,
Summer, who wants no more Tuesdays

P.S. *I hope you can forgive me.*

November 30

Dear Metti,

I was at my dad's yesterday. I couldn't stand being there for very long, so Mom came and picked me up. I hadn't even told him I was leaving. I just texted my mom to come get me. So, as I was leaving, Dad asked me not to leave so soon because he wanted to have some time with me.

I turned around so fast, gunning him down with a killer stare, and told him he should have thought about having time with me before signing up for California! WOW! I'm kind of proud for saying something to my dad. It's been getting harder lately to stand up for myself. I don't know why; it just is.

Both my parents froze in shock. For the most part, I don't get attitude. But when I do, every negative energy snaps out like a striking alligator ready to devour. By the look on my parents' faces, I guess I was ready to devour.

My dad is a big boy. He can handle it. When I said this to my mom, she asked me if I'm ready to handle it.

There's no way my mom has a disease in her brain. How can someone like that come up with such wise stuff to say?

Signed,
Summer, who doesn't know much anymore

December 1

Dear Metti,

First day back to school from the Thanksgiving holiday. Everybody was out of it, including the teachers. I feel like such a robot. I moved throughout my day, going through the motions. The bell rings, go to class, sit in class, take notes, the bell rings, go to the next class, and so on and so on. At lunch, I hardly talked to anyone. It's funny (not really), but friends from before are just pleasant faces in the crowd. I'm not friendless, but I'm not with friends either. Does that make any sense?

Signed,
Summer, who can't make sense of anything

December 2

Dear Metti,

My mom told me she tried waking me up from my nap yesterday to have our Tuesday Time, but I was too sleepy and very grumpy.

I totally forgot—and how can we keep doing Tuesday Time when all of this is going on? She said that we could catch up next Tuesday. I felt bad and mad at the same time. How am I supposed to live my life? Like normal? How?

Signed,
Summer. That's just it: Summer

December 4

Dear Metti,

Forrest went back to college. He gets a longer break at Christmas time. I miss him. It gets hard being the only one around with Mom all the time.

Today, she kept forgetting what day it was. I must have told her a zillion times that today is Friday. Two minutes later, she would ask what day it was.

She couldn't find her glasses. This has always been a problem for her. Now, it's just worse. I found them for her and gave them to her, and minutes later, she asked me if I'd seen her glasses. I got so stressed out because this all happened as I was going out the door to get to school. Well, again, I missed the bus, so again, Mom had to take me. Half the time, she forgets where she's going. The other half of the time, she forgets how to get there. I'm headed for ISS for being late for school too many times. I had a test in English today, and I wouldn't be surprised if I spelled my own name wrong!

Signed,
Summer, who's stressed out

December 5

Dear Metti,

It's Saturday. I'm at my dad's to see if I can make some peace with him. We are busy packing, and Forrest will be around later this afternoon. Dad says he has a surprise for me. I'm not thrilled, but I'm good about it and trying to look somewhat happy. Truthfully, I'm a bit curious, but mostly terrified. Oh, well, I'll wait and see. Got to go help pack pots and pans. Yeah! What fun!

Signed,
Summer the professional packer (not)

December 6

Dear Metti,

   Back home with Mom. She looks so tired and wrung out. She reminded me of her doctor's appointment coming up on the 10th. I am going with her. How much more exciting can my life get?

Signed,
Summer, who doesn't like doctors

December 8

Dear Metti,

Today is Tuesday. You know, it's funny how my mom remembers when it's Tuesday but gets all confused with the other days of the week.

Mom says that we're staying home for this one. I was looking forward to going out and doing something. Lately that's all I want to do: get out of the house. Oh, well, staying home it is. Oh, by the way, I didn't do so good on that English test. I did spell my name right, but I was close to a flunking grade.

December 8 (later)

Dear Metti,

For our Tuesday Time, we made gingerbread houses. I hadn't made one of those in a long time. We had graham crackers, gum drops, homemade frosting, pretzel sticks, and lots of M&Ms. My house came out looking like something from a demented cartoon. My mom's, on the other hand, looked like the classic Hansel and Gretel house. I totally hate that story. Why would any parent want to read to their child a story about child abusers and murders?

I asked my mom if she ever read Hansel and Gretel to me as a kid. She said, "Summer, I'm a librarian. Do the math." She'd read it to me several times. One time was during my fourth birthday party. The big activity of my party was making gingerbread houses, so to go along with the theme, Mom read Hansel and Gretel. Well, a mother of one of my little friends yelled at my mom for reading such an awful story. My mom calmly assured her that Hansel and Gretel expose children to German folklore, which can be found in the Grimm Brothers' fairy tales. At times, it's such a drag to have a librarian as a mom. Thank goodness I was too young to understand that yet.

For Mom's memory book, I took a picture of the houses and wrote, "Living in a sweet neighborhood." Gotta keep the humor going, no matter how sad we all are.

Signed,
Summer, who wants to know: Who in the world are the Grimm Brothers?

147

December 10

Dear Metti,

Well, well, well, there is an advantage to going with Mom to her doctor's appointments. I get out of school early. Mom says it isn't going to be that way all the time. Hey, sometimes works for me.

It wasn't as bad as I thought it was going to be. In fact, I have a ton to share with you.

The office where Mom sees the doctor is actually really comfy and nice. Mom and I sat on a puffy tan couch. The walls were painted a beautiful, swirly blue, like dancing water. There was this hushing noise in the background they called "white noise." Like noise has a color. Whatever. The rug was thick enough to be a mattress. I met Dr. Walters, who looked rather young to be a doctor. I hope she's old enough to know what she's doing. Her first name is Priscilla, which I thought was a pretty name, especially for a doctor.

We spent most of the time reviewing Mom's file. Dr. Walters kept encouraging us to ask questions and share things about what's been going on at home. Mom said she was good with understanding things. She says that routine is helpful. She shared that forgetting things drives her insane. She loses patience with herself. It was hard for me to hear her say things like that, but at the same time, it was good to finally talk about it.

Dr. Walters suggested carrying a little notebook around with very basic but important information. Write in it the dates, the season, any upcoming holidays, and the order of the day's events to help keep her on track.

Dr. Walters asked my mom how her work was going. I hadn't even thought about that. I know how much I'm out of it in school; I can't imagine how it is for Mom at work. But Mom said that she can manage for the most part. Some of her coworkers are getting a little worried because, at times, Mom does stupid things that get their attention.

Then Dr. Walters asked, "How are you doing, Summer?"

I wasn't prepared for this. Why was she asking me about me? This was Mom's appointment, and this was Mom's doctor, so what did any of that have to do with me?

"Things are fine," I said. I looked at my mom, and my mom looked back at me, shaking her head no.

Dr. Walters noticed this. "Clearly, Mom disagrees, so why not take a stab at it and share with me the life and times of April and Summer Whitcomb?" I have to hand it to Dr. Walters: she has a powerful calm about her, so I took the stab.

It was like the time Forrest and I talked at the restaurant. I started off slow, but then got talking faster and faster to a point where I had to pause to get air. The whole time I was talking, Dr. Walters just sat and listened. She didn't interrupt me. And my mom was totally chill. She didn't make a single judgmental expression. When I was done sharing, it felt like a boulder the size of Texas had rolled off my shoulders. I felt like I could breathe better.

Dr. Walters leaned in like she was going to tell us a secret. "Telling it like it is helps more than anything when dealing with Alzheimer's disease. Basically, reality is distorted enough for a person with Alzheimer's. If the people they trust cover up or sugar-coat what is actually happening, it just adds to the distortion of their reality. So, if the lost car keys are found in the bag of dry dog food, that's the way it is. Don't belittle it by saying something else."

Toward the end of the appointment, Dr. Walters handed each of us a pamphlet describing the support groups we could join. Mom said she would think about it. But by her tone, it sounded more like "thanks but no thanks."

I said I might be interested in it. Anyway, my first meeting is on December 30th. My group meets every Wednesday evening from seven to nine in the basement of the same building as Dr. Walter's office. Mom's group meets there too, but on Thursday evenings. When Mom realized this, she announced, "Thank goodness it isn't on a Tuesday." You got to hand it to my mom for remembering her Tuesdays!

Signed,
Summer, who sees a bit of light
at the end of the tunnel

December 12

Dear Metti,

I'm at my dad's. Forrest and I had a long talk after Dad went to bed. I couldn't believe it: we talked until two in the morning. I told him about being with Mom during her appointment. Bonus for me: getting out of school early. Forrest would be mortified leaving school while it was still in session. He said I should join the support group. As he put it, "What do you have to lose?" He thinks I could use the support, being home alone with Mom and all.

Forrest thinks Mom should go to her group as well. He asked me what I thought. I agreed with him. What can it hurt for Mom and me to have others to talk to and share with in hopes of gaining some support?

Maybe my mom is afraid. Maybe being around other people with Alzheimer's scares her because it shows her what she might look like to others, like her coworkers, her boss, the neighbors, and especially me. Forrest thought that was pretty good insight for a 13-year-old! (Either that, or I was delusional because it was after midnight.)

Metti, I'm good with joining this support group. In fact, I'm looking forward to it. I have no idea what it will be like, but I'm good with it.

Signed,
Summer, who sees a bit more light
at the end of the tunnel

December 13

Dear Metti,

I'm home from my dad's. When I got here, Mom was way out of it. I came home to her crying because she had spilled coffee on her wedding dress. She was standing there in her white bathrobe that she's had for a million years. I talked her through it, just like what Dr. Walters said to do. I told it like it is. There was no coffee on her wedding dress. She had spilled some on her bathrobe. Over and over, I said, "BATHROBE!" until she finally seemed to get it and calmed down.

Signed,
Summer, who can't wait
for this support group

December 15

Dear Metti,

It's almost scary that it's Tuesday already. Some weeks go so slow, while other weeks like this one just fly. It's my turn to pick the activity. And I have totally no idea what to do. I'll think about it while I'm in school.

December 15 (later)

Dear Metti,

Well, during math class, I had a brainstorm as to what to do for our Tuesday Time. I just hope she likes it. Please don't think I'm being rude to my mom, but I don't want to go out as much anymore. What happens if she has one of her "spells" in public? Okay, I know this is bad of me, but I would feel better if I had someone with us instead of just Mom and me when we go out.

So I planned a night of movies. Not any movies, but movies that she grew up with as a teenager. This planning meant I have to go to the library after school to get the movies because I'm still afraid to illegally download movies without Forrest supervising, and none of them were on Netflix. I did some Googling and picked out two good movies. They're old, but I think she'll still like them.

Signed,
Summer, who likes old movies?

December 16

Dear Metti,

My movie night with Mom was a hit! We laughed, we cried, and we stuffed ourselves with popcorn. Mom howled when Harrison Ford came on the scene in "Raiders of the Lost Ark." She remembered how the last song in "The Breakfast Club" gets her choked up. She totally enjoyed watching not one, but two of the movies I picked out. I was surprised I wasn't too bored. Not bad for old movies.

Signed,
Summer the "old" movie buff

December 17

Dear Metti,

Dad called me today to remind me that he had a surprise for me. I said, "Yeah, okay." (Over the years since the divorce, I don't get too hyped over surprises from my dad. He's not the reliable type when it comes to surprises.) He firmly told me to be home right after school tomorrow. So now he has me wondering. Maybe I'm getting a puppy, and he wants to be sure I'm home when he brings it.

Signed,
Summer the potential puppy owner
P.S. *If a puppy is his surprise, he's done GOOD!*

December 19

Dear Metti,

Did my dad ever SCORE! He gave me a BOMB of a surprise!!!!!!! My dad took me, Forrest, and Clara Rose (still can't believe Forrest has the same girlfriend) to a Journey concert!!!!!!!! I LOVE THIS BAND!!!!!!!! Our seats were crazy good!!!!!!!!!

At one point, Steve Perry looked right at me while he was performing out on the extended stage area. Forrest said he was looking my direction because it was Clara Rose he was looking at and not me. How would I know anyway, closing my eyes and holding my breath? What can I say? I was nervous.

They sang all of my favorites, like "Street Lights," "Faithfully," "Anyway You Want It," "Wheel in the Sky," and "Open Arms." I bawled during "Open Arms." I couldn't help thinking about my mom and her Alzheimer's. It almost was as if it was being sung as kind of a theme song for my mom. I wonder if she knew about Dad's surprise. She loves Journey too. Like, who doesn't LOVE JOURNEY?! I got to scream and dance and be a crazy fan all night long. It felt good. I had fun chillin' with Clara Rose and even with my dad. BUT the best was when Steve Perry looked at ME!!!!!!!!

Signed,
Summer, who knows he looked at her!

December 20

Dear Metti,

This is one of the last times I'll be at my dad's apartment with him here. Dad agreed that Forrest could stay until the end of the school year. This came as a big relief to Forrest. Things have a way of working out, even if it is during rough times. Forrest will have his associate's degree, so he doesn't have to worry about not being able to finish his first two years. Next fall, he can apply to any college he wants to continue with his engineering degree. If you ask me, he's thinking of staying in the area because Clara Rose has a year to go before moving on to another college. They seem serious. But what do I know?

I'm feeling better about my dad moving to California. I still think that he's ditchin' us, but I'm not as mad about it as I was. Maybe it'll make things a bit easier. You know, not having to go back and forth on weekends and stuff like that. Metti, there are days like today when I feel strong about everything, and then all of a sudden, I feel so weak and overwhelmed.

I'm supposed to go with Mom to her doctor's appointment on Tuesday. I guess this is something I have to get used to doing with her. By the way, our support groups start next week. I'm kind of nervous about going to that, too. What happens if they expect you to share about your life? You know, stuff that happens between my mom and me. I want to know about other kids like me and how they handle it. So much going on in my life. . .

Signed,

Summer, who is emotionally all over the place

December 21

Dear Metti,

   Mom is at it again. I poured my cereal this morning and out came a box prize for sure!!!! Mom's watch.

Signed,
Summer the cereal box winner

December 22

Dear Metti,

Mom's appointment went fine. Dr. Walters went over some medicine stuff. I tuned her out because that white noise was putting me to sleep.

"Are you planning on attending the support groups I recommended?" she asked.

I told her, "Yes and no."

"Why 'no'?"

I told her I'm not good at feeling pressured to share when things get personal. As the group goes around the circle, I don't want to be expected to share just because it's my turn. I want to be able to share and talk about stuff when I want to talk about it.

Dr. Walters assured me that no one shares unless they totally feel comfortable. You don't even have to answer a question if you don't want to. You just say "pass." However, at some point, some sharing must take place, because that's the only way you can truly get support from others, and that's how they get support from you.

Mom still didn't look too keen on the idea. Dr. Walters noticed this and asked, "What are your thoughts on attending your group?"

My mom just said, "Pass."

Signed,
Summer the Support Groupie (get it?)

P.S. *Mom said that we'll do our Tuesday Time next week.*
She'll be in charge of the activity.

December 24

Dear Metti,

It's Christmas Eve, and we always go to the Christmas Eve service. I guess I never told you about believing in God and going to church. Mom and I go more than Forrest does. My dad going to church? Not on your life.

Anyway, the candlelight service is my absolute favorite service. We got there early, so when the whole church was lit up by candlelight, I got a good view. I love singing Christmas hymns. It's safe to say that Christmas is my favorite time of year. I don't say this just because I like getting presents (though that helps). It's my favorite time of year because I love Christmas lights, the food, and decorating.

After church, we changed into comfy clothes, ate glazed doughnuts with warm cider, and watched *A Christmas Carol*. Before going to bed, we put baby Jesus in his cradle and picked out the present we want to open first on Christmas morning. My dad will be coming over at about 10:00 tomorrow morning. Forrest and I will make Mom breakfast in bed, and then PRESENT TIME!!!!

Signed,
Summer, WHO LOVES CHRISTMAS!!!!!

December 26

Dear Metti,

Christmas was the bomb! I got lots of cool clothes, which I needed because I'm growing like all over. I'm getting taller, getting hips, and YES, even getting some boobs! So I look good in my new clothes. I fill out my shirts, and I have a smooth shape in my tight jeans. My mom loved the perfume I got her; from Forrest, she got an umbrella decorated with books; and from the both of us, we gave her a gift certificate to a bookstore in the mall. She's totally happy.

I gave Forrest a silly-looking coffee mug with a note inside inviting him to go out for coffee sometime. Forrest gave me a sweet-looking backpack for school or whatever I want to use it for. Then from my mom, I got the movies Cinderella and Lady and the Tramp on DVD. When I was a little girl, I would watch these movies over and over on VHS. With the movies, Mom wrote a note saying, "I love watching movies with you. Let's have old movie night again real soon." I gave her a hug and told her old movie night anytime is fine with me.

The last gift I opened was from my dad. This is what made Christmas the bomb! Usually I don't like getting expensive gifts as a way of showing love. But I know my dad, and his way is his way, so I go with it. Well, he gave me a Journey t-shirt, a Journey poster signed by the band, and a poster of Steve Perry with the words, "To Summer: keep following your dreams." I screamed, hugged my dad, and screamed some more. I ran upstairs changed into my shirt. I ran back downstairs to get the masking tape. Ran back upstairs and hung up my two posters! On the wall facing my bed are my Journey men.

My dad and I are getting along maybe the best we ever have, and it's weird because it's right before he's leaving for California. I shared this with my mom, and she'd forgotten that he was moving. Even though she forgets things, she still has wise words to share: "Summer, better that you have these few good memories of getting along with your dad than none at all. None of us live forever." Then she cocked her head and asked if what she had said made any sense, because she was losing memory of what she was saying. I told her she is the wisest person I know.

Merry Christmas to all! "God bless us, everyone." Tiny Tim (I think). Charles Dickens at his best.

Signed,
Summer, who has one more
Christmas Wish--SNOW!

December 29

Dear Metti,

Our Tuesday Time was today. I have to hand it to my mom. We had a Journey night. She totally shocked me when she showed up for dinner wearing a Journey shirt of her own. So I went and changed into my Journey shirt. There we were, eating pizza in our shirts, listening to their music and talking about which band member we would marry—back in the day, of course. Afterward, we had a Journey dance off. Just as we were really getting into it, Forrest came home with Clara Rose. All four of us were dancing around in our own styles, like square dancers gone rebels. I grabbed the camera and snapped pictures. This night was a memory-maker, and I have pictures to put in Mom's book.

Signed,
Summer, who thinks Mom is just
fine (even her dancing)

December 30

Dear Metti,

Tonight is my first time at my support group. Yeah, I'm a bit nervous. Like, what if the other kids are already friends? Here I come, the new kid having to break in. I don't know about this. At the time, it sounded like a good idea, but now I'm not so sure. I'll write you about it later.

Not much else happening. Going to bed real late (2:15 am) and getting up real late (11:30 am). Hey, that's what holiday breaks are for.

Signed,
Summer, who isn't so sure
about support groups

December 31

Dear Metti,

Oh, I have so much to write to you about. My support group meeting went pretty good. There're six of us total, and it happens to be three guys and three girls. So it makes it nice and even.

The facilitator's name is Lindsey. She's 27 and married, and has a baby boy named Noble. She's about the same height as me. She has very long, walnut-brown hair. Lindsey is the real deal. She's not fake. She knows how to keep our group in balance. She knows how to set boundaries for the sake of everyone in the group. At the same time, she allows you to express your thoughts and feelings in your own time and space. It turns out, Lindsey's mom had early-onset Alzheimer's disease. She's been on the journey before, so she feels like our guide. I like her. She seems very level-headed with her advice.

I can't write about everybody in this one entry. I'll write about the two girls, then I'll write about the three guys later. I know stuff about them because tonight was a time of just hanging out and getting to know each other.

I'll start with Chloe. She's the youngest of the group at age 12 in sixth grade. She's like everybody's little sister. She's a bit small for her age, but she makes up for it in some of the things she says. So in that sense, she's mature for her age. She's an only child, adopted by older parents. She was born somewhere in South America but doesn't remember anything about her baby years because she was very young when she got adopted. She has almond eyes with hair as dark as black licorice. It's her mom who has Alzheimer's.

The other girl, besides me, is Paige. She's 13 years old and in eighth grade. She has three older brothers, who tease her as much as they protect her. I seem to click with her the most. I know it's kind of early to tell, but it just seems that way. She likes some of the same stuff I do. She loves the beach, movies that make her cry, and journaling as her way of dealing with her dad's Alzheimer's. She appears pretty logical in how she handles things. She has blonde hair with candy-green eyes. She plays on her school's tennis team.

I'll tell you about the guys when I write again. I told Mom I'd help her paint her bedroom. I'm totally psyched, because after we paint her room, I get to paint my room! So, off to the paint store we go to pick out colors and have fun designing. (I'm thinking of becoming an interior decorator. What do you think?)

Signed,
Summer the future interior decorator?

P.S. *This is my last time writing to you this year!*

January 1

Dear Metti,

Happy New Year!!!!! We had a party of sorts. Forrest came over without Clara Rose. She had to be with her family because her grandma is in the hospital. Dad did make it. He wasn't sure if he would because of all the stuff he had left to do before moving day.

So it was the four of us. Just like old times before their divorce. Mom, Dad, and Forrest made a toast with pretty pink wine. Oh my gosh, it looked so fresh and fruity. Mom let me have a little from her glass. My fancy drink was a BoBa smoothie. We watched the ball drop in like seventy-thousand different places. Every news station was covering different counties bringing in the New Year. In such-n-such county, they drop a huge rose. In another county, they drop an oversized lollipop. In another county, they drop a 500-pound chocolate bar. (I wouldn't mind being there when that hits the ground.)

Here in Mountville, we drop a big old shoe. It drops from our tallest building in the town square, the old Fitchenberg Shoe Company. The building has been converted into condos, but back a hundred years or so, Mountville was known worldwide for its high-quality shoes, made by the Fitchenberg brothers. So, what the heck, our county drops a shoe.

By 1:00 am, we all were in bed except for Dad; he drove home. Forrest crashed in his old bedroom. It felt good having him asleep in the room next to mine. It was a nice time. Wouldn't you know, we're all getting along, and Mom has something wrong with her and Dad is moving to California. Yep, just another day in the life of my "normal" family. I'm ready to change the subject. Moving right along.

Remember how I told you I'd write about the guys in my support group? Let me start with Jonathan. He's the oldest in the group at 15. He's in tenth grade. He's tall, really skinny, and plays basketball all the time. It isn't just his favorite sport; it's his outlet in dealing with his mom's Alzheimer's. His dad is taking his mom's condition pretty hard. At times, Jonathan feels like he has to be a dad to his dad. He's an only child, which makes it even harder. He has a cousin nearby who helps out some with having company. Jonathan is also the senior of the group; he's been in the group the longest.

Eric is the shyest out of everybody. He has it tough. Both his parents died in a car accident. For the past seven years, he's been living with his mom's sister, his Aunt Sarah. First, he lost both his parents, and now his Aunt Sarah has Alzheimer's. He's 14 and in ninth grade. He's pretty smart but doesn't like to show it. He has hair any girl would die for—thick, curly brown hair. He isn't sure where he can go when his aunt's Alzheimer's gets bad. His aunt never married, so there's no uncle around to take care of him. I really feel for him. I know my dad is going to be on the other side of the country. But I still have a dad and an older brother. I'm a bit scared, now, thinking about how things are going to work out if I'm left without my mom.

Jackson Thomas, who goes by JT, is 13 years old and in eighth grade. He's like me in that his parents are divorced. He has an older sister and a younger one. JT feels left out, being in the middle of two girls. I see him gravitating toward Jonathan as an older brother type. His mom has Alzheimer's. His dad has been getting back into their lives since his mom's diagnosis. (Lucky JT and his dad have a chance to grow closer. While my dad is moving farther away. This whole thing with my dad has me so confused.) JT's family is pretty rich. His dad owns a business that's been in the family for seventy years. JT is expected to take his dad's place when he retires. JT doesn't want anything to do with it. His passion is music. He plays five different instruments. His favorite is the trumpet. He plays trumpet in the school's marching band. Music is his therapy and escape. He has stallion black hair with intense brown eyes. He shares the least, but I'm guessing he feels the most.

I think this group will be helpful for me. One of the questions Lindsey asked everyone was, "What do you see this group doing for you?"

All of us answered in basically the same way: "For us to get close enough to really be there for each other."

Maybe my mom will get involved with her support group if she sees how it can be helpful. Time will tell. (Something my parents would say. Ugh!!!!!)

Signed,
Summer, who is willing to give it a go

January 2

Dear Metti,

Mom and I had a rough day. We were painting Mom's bedroom when everything got crazy for her. She stopped painting and left the room. I followed her into the upstairs bathroom and found her crying. I asked her what was wrong. She said that everything was going wrong. And she felt bad for bringing me into it all, but she didn't remember even agreeing to this painting job in the first place. What was really making her upset was we weren't getting paid for all our hard work. What the heck?

I explained to her that we were painting her bedroom in our very own house, nobody else's. We didn't need to get paid because we wanted to paint our own bedrooms. And I was glad to help her paint. She looked at me and said that she didn't remember wanting to paint her bedroom. Then she really started crying because she didn't even remember picking out this ugly paint. I tried to comfort her by saying that Water Lily Green is a beautiful color. Her favorite color is green. But my mom didn't remember that, either.

Metti, I looked at my mom in the mirror standing right next to me. She looked so lost, like a misplaced rag doll. Her eyes were heavy from being overwhelmed. Her arms sagged like two messy, braided pigtails. It's really hard for me to see my mom so lost, so confused, so forgetful. Every curve of her body was shaking off the fear. Before I could break, I skipped back into her bedroom and vigorously started to paint. With each stroke I kept repeating in my head, "My mom is going to be okay. My mom is going to be okay." At this point, I'm really not sure what else to do.

Signed,
Summer, who prays that
her mom will be okay

January 4

Dear Metti,

Back to school from a long break. I touched base with some friends. Well, if you can call them that. I have friends I can talk to in school, but out of school, I don't really have anybody.

In history class, our normal teacher is out for a week. He broke his leg skiing. Kind of wish that was the case with me. (Then I'd have another week off from school.)

Signed,
Summer, who has never skied,
so I'd probably break my leg trying to do it

January 5

Dear Metti,

I AM SO MAD!!!!!!!!!!!!!!!!!!!! I literally can't even write. I hate her!!!!! How could she do this to me? I hate her!!!!! She's not my mom. She's a witch. She is mean and cruel, and I hate her! Metti, do you get it? I hate her!!!! She had no right to go into my room! She had no right to ruin my stuff! I HATE HER!!!!!!

Signed,
Summer, who HATES HER MOTHER!!!!!!!!!!!!!!!!!!!!!!

January 6

Dear Metti,

I'm not writing. I hate her. She wanted me to go to school, and I screamed at her as loud as I could. I slept with my door locked. She will never get into my room again. I will lock her out of my life. I have to, because she can't be trusted. She isn't my mother. She has an evil force living inside of her, and it will come out and hurt me. She had no right to do what she did! I didn't go to school. I kept my door locked so she couldn't come in. She needs to go away. I need to go away.

Signed,
Summer, who doesn't care anymore

January 7

Dear Metti,

I hate her.

Signed,
Summer, who wants revenge

January 8

Dear Metti,

She is evil, and I'm going to get even with her.

Signed,
Summer, who has a plan for revenge

January 9

Dear Metti,

I got even with her. She'll know about it when she comes home from work today. She'll find out, just like I did when she did it to me! Fair is fair. I still hate her.

Signed,

Summer, who knows her mom deserves it

January 9 (later)

Dear Metti,

My revenge plan worked. My mom came home, went into her bedroom, and SCREAMED!!!!!! She screamed the loudest I've ever heard her scream, so I knew I got even with her. Good. She got what she had coming to her!!!!!!

Signed,
Summer, who feels no guilt

January 10

Dear Metti,

Now Mom has taken it too far. Guess who showed up for lunch today? Forrest. Oh, Mom went behind my back and called him to come home for a visit, and I'm supposed to be okay with that? Not after what she's done to me.

Just as I thought, Forrest wanted to talk to me after lunch. Big brother in his sickening, logical way suggested we go for a walk. Okay, I decided to play this game because I could tell him what Mom did, he'd be on my side, and Mom will lose to the both of us! We walked to the local park.

"Why are you so mad at Mom?" Forrest asked. "And why did you write 'I hate you' all over her bedroom walls?" Then before I knew it, he started to really lay into me about it.

So I let the world have it!!!!!!! I told Forrest that fair is fair, an eye for eye, and she deserved it—so don't come preachin' to me! AND Forrest didn't even know what she had done to me; he thought I was the immature one. I was getting mad all over again. Finally, I yelled at him to just shut up and have some emotion for once in his life. I TOLD him. I told him what Mom did to me.

Last Tuesday, I came home from school thinking about how, for our Tuesday Time, we were going to start painting my room. When I entered my room, I walked into something horrible! Something so awful! All over the floor were pieces of ripped-up paper. I looked at my walls. I looked at my ugly, stark, naked walls.

SHE RIPPED UP MY JOURNEY POSTERS!!!!!!! She had no right to do that!!!!! She ripped them up because she didn't want those men's eyes looking at me!!!!!!! Metti, she ripped up my posters!!!!! She thought that their eyes were going to be looking at me!!!!! THEY WERE MY POSTERS!!!!!!

Dad gave them to me. Those posters were a memory maker for me. That concert night was one of the few cool times I've had with Dad and Forrest. Mom destroyed my poster that had been signed by the band, and my favorite Steve Perry poster. Steve had written, "To Summer: keep following your dreams."

MY MOM HAS RUINED THAT MEMORY FOREVER!!!!!! She is forbidden to come in my room. I yelled, I screamed, I cursed, and I cried! Forrest remained silent. He just let me be.

Forrest guided me over to the monkey bars. We climbed up and sat on top. He asked me if I remembered how we used to play castle. I confessed that I did remember, and how that game used to scare me so much. We used to pretend alligators were swimming around on the ground, so we had to run to the monkey bars and climb up as fast as we could and sit on top to be safe.

"Summer, Mom has Alzheimer's. Just like we got so involved with our make-believe play about alligators swarming us. Mom truly thinks that eyes on a poster could be looking at you, because that's the effect Alzheimer's has on a person. The Alzheimer's is her alligators."

Oh, all of this Alzheimer's stuff had gone too far with me.

I told him, "It's Mom's fault she has Alzheimer's. If she had taken better care of herself like Dad does, she wouldn't have this disease!" I told him, "Alzheimer's can't be an excuse for everything, because it's not FAIR!"

Forrest shot me a look to kill. Then he was the one yelling. "Summer, Mom can't help having Alzheimer's! You think this is easy for her? Do you think she made a wish to a magic genie to get Alzheimer's? SHE CAN'T HELP IT!!!! Any more than you can help it from getting a stomach virus or a bad cold. Does Mom get all mad at you for getting sick? No, because you can't help it. Or can you? Take better care of yourself, Summer! Come on, you should take better care of yourself. I'm in Mom's corner on this one, all the way. You are being totally selfish, Summer Ray Whitcomb!"

Forrest took some deep breaths as he wiped his sleeve across his face. He never cries. I was shook. Forrest never yells either. He is always in control, always logically resolving things with little emotion tied to it.

Without any warning, he grabbed my glasses off my face and yelled some more. "Summer, you should have taken better care of your eyes because then you wouldn't need glasses!" Then he yanked my mouth open. "Summer, you should have taken better care of your teeth because then you wouldn't need braces! I don't hear you saying that about yourself! Like can you help it?"

I pushed his hands off of my face. He didn't hurt me physically. What got hurt was my pride. My stupid, stupid pride. I hate this Alzheimer's disease. It really is an evil thing who enjoys poisoning my mother's thought process. Now look what it is doing to the way I'm thinking toward my own mother. I knew he was right. I knew I was totally wrong.

We sat in silence. The kind of silence you really feel, like at the end of a haunted house ride. You know, after all the screaming and surprises are done everything goes into a thick dark silence while your heart pounds and your nerves have to have time to settle.

Quietly, Forrest apologized for yelling and yanking at my face. Even more quietly, I apologized for my behavior. I asked him if Mom knew why I was so mad at her. He said she didn't have a clue. "She doesn't remember doing anything to you, so when she read those words on her walls, she freaked out and called me."

I felt so horrible. I felt so horrible that I nearly threw up. Luckily, I didn't. (It would have been pretty gross to witness vomit falling all the way down from the top of the monkey bars.)

We walked home in a more soothing kind of silence. As soon as I entered the house, I ran to my mom and hugged her like I had never hugged her before. I sobbed into her shoulder, telling her that I don't just want her in my life, I NEED her in my life. Over and over, I told her that I didn't hate her.

Mom hugged me back. Forrest helped me paint over my hate messages on Mom's walls. I still have a Journey shirt, and that is good enough for me.

Signed,
Summer, who doesn't deserve her mother

January 12
Dear Metti,

Mom and I had to share our Tuesday Time today with Dad. He flies out to California this Saturday the 16th. All of his stuff is leaving by moving truck on Thursday and Friday. Dad flies out Saturday, and it's all over. After Saturday, it'll be all done. My dad will officially live in California.

So, we went out to eat at my choice of restaurant. It was awkward. I could sense that Mom and I were still on the mend from our fight. And I had no idea what to talk about with Dad because next time I see him will be. . . whenever. What do you say to someone who is leaving you during a very emotional and complicated time in your life?

There won't be weekend visits anymore. I'm not close to my dad, but just knowing he is in the same state as me gives me some connection with him. After Saturday, he'll be on the other side of the country. We made plans to see him off on Saturday.

That's it. There's not much else to write about.

Signed,
Summer, who doesn't want all of
this going on in her life

January 13

Dear Metti,

Group really made me feel good tonight. Everyone gave me a "friendly" hard time about missing last week. I told them I couldn't make it because I was locked in my room. I didn't think they would, like, realize that I'd been missing, but they did. So, I had to talk about the whole experience all over again.

At first, I thought they would think I had acted like a baby. Surprisingly, they understood where I was coming from. Each of them shared a time when something important to them got ruined. We all couldn't help laughing at Paige's story in particular.

When Paige was in kindergarten, a boy who had a crush on her made her a fancy egg out of clay. Paige kept this egg on her desk at home, just as something special from her childhood. One day, when she came home from school, the egg wasn't on her desk. She searched everywhere in her room but couldn't find it. That evening, when she went into the refrigerator, there was her special egg. She pulled it out, showing it to her mother. Her mom said that Paige's dad was convinced the egg was real and must be kept in the refrigerator, not on her desk.

I asked Paige how she dealt with her dad's confusion. Turns out, she has a plan to make another egg just like her special childhood one. Without her dad knowing, she'll make the switch, and all will be good.

But what about when something is ruined for good? JT says that he just pays for a new one of whatever got ruined, broken, or lost. Easy solution for him because he has the money.

Lindsey suggested putting things in a locked box or trunk. "But I know," she said, "that doesn't work for pictures on your walls or decorations on your shelves," Instead, she suggested I tape a message next to each poster identifying it. She made an example of my poster experience. If I get new posters for my birthday, I could tape a message next to them saying how these are special people to me. This way, logic has a fighting chance of overriding the hallucinations. It's not a guarantee, but maybe it will help.

Signed,

Summer, who needs this support group

January 14

Dear Metti,

Dad came by again to spend some time with me. We went
out for ice cream, just the two of us. We talked about small
stuff. I feel like I'm floating on top of a cloud, just inches off
the ground. I know people say that when they're in love. I'm
saying it because I feel like I'm in such a daze.

Signed,
Summer the Cloud Rider

January 15

Dear Metti,

Dad took us out for Chinese. This time it was all four of us. It went okay. We all joked about the fortunes in our fortune cookies. Dad said something about coming to see him when I have a holiday break. I'm not even thinking that far ahead.

He wanted to be sure I would be at the airport 9:00 sharp to see him off. I told him I'd be there. It's all good. Like, it has to be.

Signed,
Summer, who hates airports
even more than California

January 16

Dear Metti,

Just like that, my dad is gone. Off to California, and no looking back. We hugged, and I think his eyes got teary. He even hugged my mom and told her to take care. That's when I lost it and cried really hard. He didn't mean it to be sarcastic. He actually said it like he still cares about my mom. My mom, you got to admit, can be one sassy lady. She told him to take care but passed on hugging him back. Forrest teared up as he shook Dad's hand and gave him a guy kind of hug. Then off he went, not taking any one of us with him.

Signed,
Summer, who is so glad
this part is over with

January 19

Dear Metti,

For our Tuesday Time, we did something I haven't done since elementary school—coloring. Yep, my mom bought some Disney character coloring books and two new packs of crayons, and we colored. Afterward, she hung my pictures on the refrigerator door, just like when I was little.

Signed,

Summer, who wishes she could be five again

January 20

Dear Metti,

I had homework and Group tonight, so I'm grumpy because I'm tired. But I had to write to you. During Group tonight, some stuff was said that has me thinking.

Jonathan shared with us tonight that he had to make a decision about his future. He wants to go to college, but does he go to one nearby so he can still help out his dad? Or does he put his dreams into action and go to a college further away that he really wants to go to? Things are harder on Jonathan because he's an only child. You know, he doesn't have a sibling to help out with his dad. I can't image what that would feel like. What happens if your non-Alzheimer's parent dies before your Alzheimer's parent? Our futures are so changed by this "evil" disease.

I haven't thought much about what I'm doing or where I'm going after I graduate from high school. But having Mom the way she is, I'm naturally leaning toward being close by. Isn't it the same with teens whose parent has cancer or is disabled because of a car accident?

Too much for me to think about. My present life is changing before I'm ready for my future to begin.

Signed,
Summer, who wishes she
had a crystal ball

191

January 23 (Saturday)

Dear Metti,

I'm not at my dad's like I usually would be. He's in California.

Signed,

Summer, who hates being far away

January 24 (Sunday)

Dear Metti,

I'm still not at my dad's. He's still in California.

Signed,

Summer, who still hates being far away

January 25

Dear Metti,

There was excitement in gym class today! This girl named Michelle threw up while we were playing basketball. But that wasn't the whole thing.

Michelle told the gym teacher, Mr. Conrad, that she was feeling sick to her stomach. Well, Mr. Conrad, who is an ex-Marine, told her to suck it up and play ball. Michelle ran down the court once and threw up. So, Mr. Conrad got what was coming to him.

Meanwhile, Michelle was totally embarrassed and shouted at Mr. Conrad that it was all his fault, and told him how stupid he was for not letting her go to the nurse. Mr. Conrad got mad at her sass and sent her not to the nurse, but to the office. Word is that she threw up in the office as soon as she got there. So then Mr. Conrad was spoken to for not paying attention to what was really happening. And Michelle was spoken to about her sass to Mr. Conrad while she was puking into a trash can in the nurse's office. And the nurse was telling everybody to calm down and let the poor girl go home. What is it with ex-Marine gym teachers, anyway?

Signed,

Summer, who sure was glad not to be Michelle

January 26

Dear Metti,

   Our Tuesday Time has been postponed to this Saturday. I have no idea why or what's going on. This really could be the time Mom takes me to play bingo!

Signed,
Summer, who really doesn't need
any more anxiety in her life

January 28

Dear Metti,

Last night at Group, we talked about what we want to be when we grow up. It seemed strange talking about something so far away from now. And what we think now most likely will change a hundred times by the time we grow up.

Jonathan shared that he wants to be a professional basketball player. He wants to get a scholarship to a good college so he can play his way up through the ranks.

Chloe shared that she wants to be an actress. She takes dance and acting classes. She wants to be on Broadway. She loves how acting lets her get away from herself and her life. You know, becoming someone else for a while. This helps her get a break from her mom's Alzheimer's.

Eric shared how he's considering becoming an engineer. He's thinking about helping the environment in some way. But one thing is for sure: he wants to be married and have lots of kids.

Paige wants to go into journalism. She's thinking about doing both photography and writing. She enjoys sports, so she might become a sports writer. When she shared that with us, Jonathan told her she could cover his games when he makes it to the pros. (I think someone has a crush on someone else.)

I shared that I want to become a writer. I felt so strange after I said that. Those words sinking into the ears of everyone around me. I've never really thought about what I want to be when I grow up. Maybe I said that because I kind of am a writer now, right? I mean, I write like almost every day. How many teenagers can say that? How many adults can say that? I think I'm good with it.

Last to share was JT. He was torn up about answering because what he wants to do and what he is expected to do are not the same. JT wants to pursue music. He thinks maybe a music teacher in a high school, so he can be the band director too. But this idea won't fly with his dad because of the family business he's expected to take over.

Lindsey thanked us for sharing and told us that we all had great ideas for our lives. She told us the reason she wanted to talk about our futures is because it's for us to see beyond the here and the now, beyond the Alzheimer's. It is very important to have goals for ourselves. To have things planned for the near future (a couple of months from now), the middle future (a year or so from now), and the "long-term" future (like when we grow up).

She suggested writing some of our goals down, and then, in time, we could see how those goals changed or stayed the same. But the most important thing is to see how many of these goals we reach. So long as we are trying to go forward, the goal will always be in sight. I like Lindsey. I like what she has to say.

Signed,
Summer, who wants to be a WRITER!

January 30

Dear Metti,

Mom told me that our postponed Tuesday Time together starts at 4:00 today, so I need to be home. Then she added with a playful smile, "Oh, yeah, wear your bathing suit." Say what? (The signs are looking real good that it isn't bingo.)

Signed,
Summer, who will wear a
bathing suit any time!

January 31

Dear Metti,

It was a BLAST!!! At 4:00 yesterday, Forrest came with Clara Rose. They came walking into our house wearing flip-flops. When Forrest took off his winter coat, he didn't have a shirt on. Then he took off his sweatpants to show off his flamingo-printed bathing suit. He and Mom planned an indoor, middle-of-the-winter beach party!

We set up beach blankets and towels in the living room. Clara Rose had made sand dollar cookies. Forrest brought fancy glasses with little umbrellas to put in the drink. Mom made triple-decker sandwiches. (Get it? Sandwiches.) We played Twister and beach ball volleyball. Mom played Beach Boys music and danced like only my mom knows how to dance. Then we all relaxed to the movie Jaws. This was Forrest's idea of a good beach movie. Mom scolded him, but she let me watch it. I saw half of it from behind a pillow. Even Clara Rose hid once or twice. After the movie, we played beach-themed charades to cheer us up before calling it a night. It was good to laugh. It was good to see my mother and brother laugh. It was nice for Clara Rose to be part of it with us.

The memory objects I'm going to put into Mom's book are a flattened umbrella from her drink, a picture I drew myself of me riding on top of Jaws (the great white shark), with the words, "See, I'm not afraid of the movie Jaws!" and a made-up volleyball score card with our team winning a thousand points to two!!! (It was Clara Rose and me against Forrest and Mom.)

Signed,
Summer, who hates sharks more than ever!

February 2

Dear Metti,

Happy Groundhog Day. It happens to fall on a Tuesday, so I told Mom I'd be in charge of our Tuesday Time. It's going to be low-key by watching the movie Groundhog Day, starring Bill Murray. Maybe we'll make our traditional finger shadows on the wall.

Signed,
Summer and the groundhog, who predicted six more weeks of winter. UGH!

February 3

Dear Metti,

Group is going good. I'm getting to know everyone on a closer level than anyone at school. Tonight, we talked about how EVERYONE HATES ALZHEIMER'S! We hate how it attacks our family. We hate what it does to our loved ones. We hate how it knocks everybody else down. We hate how we have to grow up faster. We hate the fear it gives us. We hate how we have something to hate.

Lindsey suggested that we draw pictures of what we think Alzheimer's looks like. Not what it looks like on our loved one, not their confused faces, but what Alzheimer's would look like if it could pop out of their bodies. Chloe drew the best picture. She drew a picture of this evil looking figure in a trench coat, like a secret agent. She told us that she got the idea from the old movies she watches with her parents. You know, the classic evil Russian spy who almost gets away with blowing up the whole world—except for Russia, of course. Her picture showed a skinny man with yellow, bloodshot eyes. He had a very long, narrow nose that sniffed little squiggles—the vapors of fear. His long trench coat had bumps in it where he hid his guns.

"One gun is a memory gun," Chloe explained. "When you get shot with it, your memory dies, but you keep on living." She explained how his huge ears take pleasure in hearing screams of people hallucinating as they get shot by his hallucination gun. His legs were skinny as fingers. (That's because she traced her fingers to draw the legs.) On his raincoat was a badge with the name "Evil Agent A."

After we heard what Chloe had to share, we all stood up and clapped for her. Then Eric suggested that we call Alzheimer's "Evil Agent A." We all agreed.

The rest of us shared our pictures, which were totally lame compared to Chloe's. As for my picture, I drew a blackening shadow with a small head, big eyeless sockets, and a limbless body. The idea came to me from a picture of the headless horseman. (So obvious I'm the daughter of a librarian. UGH!)

Lindsey told us that giving something abstract like Alzheimer's a physical appearance can be helpful. This way, it isn't as scary, because it becomes something more tangible. It also becomes something we have more control over. We make it the way we want to make it. If we want, we can change it into looking like something else. It isn't a lot of control, but it's some. And like the old saying goes, "Any little bit helps."

I wonder what Alzheimer's would look like to my mom if I asked her to draw a picture of it. Maybe someday I'll ask her.

Signed,
Summer, who hates the "Evil Agent A"

P.S. *Exactly two months until my birthday!*

February 4

Dear Metti,

Not a good day. I forgot about a test in math. Oh, and Mom is at it again. I found 12 cans of veggies in the dryer. Why couldn't it have been money?

Signed,

Summer, who wants to find MONEY!

February 6

Dear Metti,

I did something I normally don't ever do. Go to work with my mom on a Saturday. Oh, she got so excited when I told her that I didn't feel like being home alone, so I was thinking of going to work with her. BAM!!! She screamed with shrill delight. So off to work I went with my totally delighted mother. But I made it very clear I wanted her to bring me home on her lunch break. She agreed, and out the door she skipped in total delight. (Did I mention how "delighted" she was?)

It wasn't so bad. I worked on some homework. I looked through every teen magazine. I looked through the YA section, and I even checked a book out to start reading. Oh, there's a story behind that. My mom was in the way-back of the front desk when I was checking out. She saw me and broke out into a big smile and a thumbs up! I swore I would never do it again!!!!!

Signed,
Summer, who will not grow up to be a
librarian. (No offense, Mom.)

February 8

Dear Metti,

Just thought I'd let you know that I haven't heard from my dad. Not even a phone call or a text or an email or anything. Just thought I'd let you know.

Signed,

Summer, who just needed to tell you that

February 9

Dear Metti,

Mom and I are both not feeling well. She has a migraine, and I have the stomach flu. I hate throwing up! I hate everything about it! Except that it's getting out what needs to get out SO I CAN GET BETTER!

Signed,
Summer, who needs to be
very close to a bathroom

February 11

Dear Metti,

I'm feeling better. Wow—for two days, I could only handle warm Coke. It sounds disgusting, but it was the only thing I could keep down. Today, I'm eating a full menu of crackers, Jell-O, and toast. As for my beverage, I've been promoted to chilled Coke.

Bad news is that I missed Group last night. I feel bad about it. When I'm not there, I miss the encouragement that helps me get through the week.

The good news, I guess, is that I heard from my dad today. He called around our suppertime, which isn't the same time for him because California is three hours behind us. He told me that things were crazy with the moving and starting the job. He lives in a different state but sounds the same—it's all about him. He did tell me to keep my eyes open for some mail from him. Well, I'll see what that's about. Most likely, it'll be a cheapo postcard signed by his secretary. Whatever.

Signed,
Summer, who wants her postcard
to be signed by her DAD!!!

February 13

Dear Metti,

My mail came from my dad! It's my Valentine's Day gift from him. You won't believe what he sent me. I got new Journey posters!!!!!! They aren't exactly like the ones I had before, and the poster of Steve Perry isn't signed, but I'LL TAKE IT!!!!!!!!!! I'm not sure how he found out about what happened to my first set of posters. Something tells me Forrest had something to do with it. With the posters, there's a card and a message telling me that Journey started their band in California. So getting Journey stuff there is easy. Journey has put California on the map more than the gold rush.

I hung them up and taped notes beside them. The note next to the band poster says, "These are famous authors." (Half-truth—they are authors of music.) And the message taped next to my Steve Perry poster says, "This man is Summer's special friend."

I showed it to my mom, and she didn't suspect a thing. I don't think she remembers tearing up my first set of posters. She made this comment about how she wouldn't mind having a Journey poster in her room. I just pray that this works, and they don't get destroyed a second time.

Signed,
Summer, who is a friend of Steve Perry!!!!!

February 14

Dear Metti,

Happy Valentine's Day. I made breakfast in bed for my mom. She liked the flowers I put on her tray. While I was sitting on her bed, she gave me this little jewelry box. She told me that this was her Valentine's Day gift to me. I opened it very slowly. Inside was this delicately designed ring. It was a diamond! It looked so beautiful. It looked so glittery. It looked so special. I stared at my mom in shock over the value of this ring that was for ME!

"Your birthstone is the diamond," Mom said. "I wanted to give this to you on your 16th birthday, but I can't wait that long. This ring is stocked with sentimental value. It was your great-grandmother's ring. Her birthday was April 12th. So don't be careless with wearing it. Do not wear it in a pool or at the beach in the ocean. Happy Valentine's Day!"

I leaned over to hug her, and we both tumbled deep into her thick comforter. I put it on my right-hand ring finger, and it fit just right. (I could wear it on my left ring finger to start some talk in school. But I'm not going to do that.) I'm glad she gave it to me before my 16th birthday, because knowing now what I would be getting, I couldn't have waited that long either. Thank you so very much, Mom!

Signed,

Summer, who has a rock on her hand (okay, more like a pebble)

February 16

Dear Metti,

It snowed today!!! For our Tuesday Time, we took a wonderful winter white walk. We haven't had much snow this winter, so today's snow was like walking in a landscape painting. It was falling down from the sky just perfectly. Needlepoint flakes floating effortlessly as they sewed a crystal quilt, covering the ground.

Mom and I talked about this and that. She asked me how I was doing with my dad being in California. I told her I was better now that I'd heard from him and got some mail from him. Now I know he is okay and thinking of me. Mom agreed. When we got home, we sipped on hot chocolate and went to bed early.

Signed,
Summer, who took a walk on a snowy night.
(Does Robert Frost come to mind?
Ugh! Darn this daughter-of-a-librarian curse.)

February 17

Dear Metti,

I just got back from Group. Tonight's session was very low-key. Lindsey opened up the discussion time by telling us, "Talk about whatever you feel like talking about." She wanted us to have some time just talking about normal stuff, not just stuff about Evil Agent A.

Paige started off by saying that her older brothers are driving her crazy. She feels totally suffocated by them. They don't agree on all the same things their younger sister should and shouldn't be allowed to do. So, one brother says this, and the other brother says that. Then she has her mom and dad saying something totally different. She feels like she has five people all trying to parent her at once. She looked at me and told me that she wants to come live with me. I told her that would be great! I've always wanted a sister.

Chloe chimed in by saying, "Being an only child is pretty boring." She said she would love to have any kind of sibling; it wouldn't matter who. But ideally, she'd want an older brother and a younger sister. Her older brother would look out for her, while her younger sister would do girl things with her.

JT groaned at Chloe. "No way would you want to be the middle child." JT hates being the middle child because his parents seem to focus on what "the girls" are all about and not so much on what's going on with him.

It was a good time to just talk about normal, everyday stuff. We talked a lot about school, teachers, and our favorite subjects. We talked about religion, sports, and music. Most of us believe in God; football is the favorite sport among the boys, and volleyball is the favorite sport among the girls. Our favorite bands vary as much as the flavors of ice cream we like to eat. None of us like the same music! It was good to just talk about normal, everyday teenage stuff. For next week, Lindsey told us to bring in our favorite candy bar. But I like so many!

Signed,
Summer, the Chocolate Bar Queen

February 18
Dear Metti,

A weird thing happened in school today. The fire alarms went off, and rumor was that it wasn't a drill. Somebody said that several smoke bombs went off in the library. No one knows for sure. If my mom were here, she'd think of my safety second to the safety of all those books in the library. That's my mom: all about books!

Signed,
Summer, who's going to keep
this news to herself

February 20

Dear Metti,

A most wonderful snowstorm is coming our way! My phone says it's supposed to start early Sunday morning and snow all the way through early Tuesday evening. Some stations are saying 22 to 30 inches of snow!!!!! Got to go. Mom and I have a ritual of how to prepare for storms.

Signed,
Summer, who says "LET IT SNOW!"

February 21

Dear Metti,

It's snowing, it's snowing, Old Man Winter is blowing!!!!!
Looks like no school tomorrow. Mom might even have a snow
day. She and I are ready. We have flashlights handy. We have
extra canned foods in our basement pantry. We have extra milk
and stuff in the fridge in the garage. Most importantly, we have
snacks lined up on the kitchen counter. So let it SNOW!!!!!!

Signed,
Summer, who loves a good storm

February 23

Dear Metti,

Well, I haven't had school for the past two days. Mom hasn't been to work for the last two days. We got 30 inches of snow, just as they predicted. For our Tuesday Time, we are shoveling and shoveling and shoveling. Thank goodness for our neighbor down the street. He's snow blowing everyone's sidewalks and helping dig cars out. There's such excitement in the air. Everyone is out helping each other, like one big block party.

Signed,

Summer, who still can make a snow angel

February 24
Dear Metti,

Group was cancelled due to the snow. Mom and I are going to play board games, eat our snacks, and drink hot chocolate to our heart's content. But I think there will be school tomorrow. Off to bed early.

Signed,
Summer, who is wishing for an ice storm
(since we've already had a snow storm)

February 25

Dear Metti,

Yep, we had school today.

Signed,
Summer, whose wish didn't come true--yet

February 26

Dear Metti,

My mom had a spell again. She was convinced that there was a snake in our kitchen sink. She swore she saw it. I asked her what it looked like, and she said it was a dark, slimy green with bulging eyes and a disgusting tongue. According to my mom, the snake came out, circled around the sink, and burrowed back down the drain.

Now this time, whatever she thinks she's seeing has me a bit scared. I do not like snakes. I very bravely shined a flashlight into the mouths of the double kitchen sink drains and saw nothing. To be sure, I thought of turning on the garbage disposal. Just as I reached for the switch, my mom smacked my arm and freaked out. She was scared to have chopped-up snake in her sink. Good point. . . however, a chopped-up dead snake in the sink is better than a live snake. We could call an exterminator to clean out the sink once we knew for sure the snake was dead. This plan worked with Mom.

I turned on the disposal. I let it run for a full thirty seconds. We heard nothing being chopped up. I peered down the sink hole again, and all was clear. Mom was relieved but concerned. Concerned, not because of a potential snake, but because in her brain, behind the slithering Alzheimer's, she knows it wasn't real.

Signed,
Summer the Snake Slayer

February 27

Dear Metti,

We got a surprise visit from Forrest and Clara Rose. We ordered pizza with a side of spicy hot wings. We talked and laughed about stuff. Mom was having trouble finding her words during our conversations.

Forrest looked concerned. I spoke to him quietly while getting the ice cream for dessert. I told him about the snake in the sink incident. Then his face went from concerned to shocked. He scolded me for not texting him. I assured him that I could handle it. I told him how the support group is really helping me. Then he messed up my hair and scolded me some more about the importance of calling him. I told him I'd try to do better.

Later, when I was passing the kitchen, I saw Forrest looking down the sink with a flashlight. I just had to laugh.

Signed,

Summer, who has such a gullible big brother

March 1

Dear Metti,

I heard from my dad today. He called me at 11:00 pm, not remembering how we are three hours ahead of him. He is all about California. He bragged about the warm weather (70° where he is, while we have 30 inches of snow). He bragged about the outdoor activities you can do. He even bragged about the fruit tasting better. I talked to him about school projects and visits with Forrest. Then I bragged about snow forts, snow angels, and school snow days. He was still all about California.

Signed,

Summer, who is getting cabin fever

March 2

Dear Metti,

Finally, Mom and I are going out for our Tuesday Time. We aren't sure where we're going; we're just going. After Mom comes home from work, we're getting in the car and just going. We'll see where we end up.

March 2 (later)

Dear Metti,

We ended up at the mall, but not to shop. We found ourselves playing at the arcade next to the movie theater. It has everything from pinball machines to air hockey to Skee Ball to the giant claw machines. We pretty much played on every fun machine there was to play on. I won 1,500 tickets, and Mom won 1,300 tickets. We cashed in our tickets for candy and baby-sized bouncy balls. Mom beat me at Skee Ball, and I beat her at air hockey. For a memory item to put into her book, I saved a ticket to glue to one of the pages. I'll glue candy wrappers all around the ticket.

Signed,

Summer, who wants a rematch at Skee Ball

March 3

Dear Metti,

It's exactly one month until my birthday. I can't believe that I'll be 14 years old. I feel like I just turned 13 a few months ago—not almost a year!

Tonight at Group, Lindsey was explaining to us how our parents are the same people even though they don't think or act like they used to. She said that, many times, people only see how much they're losing their loved one rather than how much they're still there. We all started getting on her case about how our parents are no way the same parents we used to have. We basically told her that she was wrong, and she had no idea what she was talking about.

Lindsey gently reminded us that she lost her mom to Evil Agent A. She told us we need to look at it as if our loved ones are ice cubes. She warned us that it would take some imagination to get the point of this. Ice cubes are solid. Ice cubes have a definite shape—a cube. Ice cubes have purpose: they keep things cold. But what happens as they melt? The structure becomes runny. The cube's shape becomes distorted. The ice cube's purpose gets weaker. Is it still an ice cube? Yes and no. Yes, because it still has some cube existence to it. It was once an ice cube, and it could be again. No, because once that ice cube is completely melted, it is no longer an ice cube.

Lindsey said that the melted ice cube is an ice cube, just in a different form. In the midst of Evil Agent A, our loved ones are still there, but in different forms. It was starting to make some sense. Chloe said that she understood the "runny" part. Her mom is found at all hours of the day, running away to the park, screaming that it's her turn on the swings.

Then Jonathan said something that got us all pretty upset. "After the ice cubes turn into water, Evil Agent A turns them into steam, evaporating them for good."

I know Jonathan means well. However, as the oldest in the group, he tends to put a death cloud over everything. Thank goodness for Lindsey. She told us that the steam becomes the memories, penetrating into our pores of life. No one evaporates in vain. There is always someone there to carry on the memories.

Metti, I don't know what I'd do without you. There are so many times that I want to talk to my mom about all the stuff said during Group. But I never know how to approach her or how she's going to take to it. She can be perfectly herself at the start of our conversation, then totally lose it three minutes later. I have to really focus on how she's still my mom, just in a different form.

Maybe I just need to simplify my words in what I'm trying to tell her. Lindsey suggested writing it down. Pass notes back and forth like we do in school. Even coloring pictures can help. Or having Mom point to pictures in a book. It seems so childish, but I'm desperate. I can't lose communication with my mom.

Lots on my brain. Got to go crash. Write to you later.

Signed,
Summer, who has a brainache

March 4

Dear Metti,

Mom sprung it on me that she had a doctor's appointment today at 4:00. I asked her why she didn't give me more notice, and the increasingly-familiar response was, "I forgot."

The appointment went fine. I could have been a million other places today. (Well, not really. I could have been chilling at home.) Like, I don't enjoy ratting on my mom in front of a doctor. They ask me things like, "How has your mother's memory been?" Or, "Is she seeing things that aren't really there?" "How's her activity? Is she still doing the normal things she has always done?"

I give the doctor generalized answers. I mean, of course Mom forgets things and sees things that aren't there and isn't sure what she's doing. But she's still my mom, and I'm not going to make her look horrible in front of a doctor.

We don't go to the doctor that often. This has been maybe my fourth time. It's all good with me as long as I have the control over how much I have to tell them. But when I talk in Group, that's a different story. Everyone in Group knows firsthand what it's like, so we understand each other. There's no judgment, no gossip, no rumors, no lies. I don't feel that way when I'm with my mom talking to the doctor. Anyway, the next doctor's appointment isn't for a while. I'm glad about that.

Signed,

Summer, who doesn't think she's going to become a doctor... ever

March 6

Dear Metti,

My dad called this morning. He asked how I was doing. I told him I was okay. He really enjoys living in California. There are lots of outdoor activities you can do year-round because of the mild weather.

He kept hinting around that, if I just say the word, he'll let me come live with him. He kept repeating the sentence, "There are lots of opportunities here for you, Summer."

I'm a teenager, not a "climb the company ladder until I'm at the top looking down on all the people I stepped on to get there," business-minded adult like my dad! He so doesn't get it. Anyway, he's doing good. I'm good that he's good. So it's all good.

Signed,
Summer, who has no interest
in opportunities in California

March 8

Dear Metti,

Forrest called today. (Wow, aren't I lucky, hearing from all the men in the family in just a few days?) He talked to Mom first, then asked for me. He told me he had a good talk with Mom.

"Has Mom had any 'incidents' lately?" he asked.

I filled Forrest in on some of the latest Whitcomb news. He was very happy to hear that I like Group. He agreed that Mom should be in a support group too. I asked about Clara Rose and stuff like that. He got really quiet about Clara Rose. So, maybe they aren't doing so great. That's all for now. Not much more to tell.

Signed,
Summer, who wants to be a bridesmaid
in her brother's wedding

P.S. *So they better not break up.*

March 9

Dear Metti,

Tuesday is here again! The week goes by so fast. For our Tuesday Time, we went to a fair. There's this huge church in town that sets up an indoor fair. They don't have rides, but they have games, vendors, and food! Mom and I pigged out on french fries, funnel cake, and cotton candy. I confess I came home feeling sick to my stomach. But it was all worth it! We walked around looking at the arts and crafts. I bought a beaded sea-blue necklace. Mom bought a recipe box. I have no idea why. She really doesn't cook or bake.

"Aunt Alice will like it for her birthday," Mom explained.

Then it made sense without really making sense. Mom's Aunt Alice has been dead for a good eight years now. I barely even remember her.

We had a good time, as a souvenir I'll print off pics I took on my phone and make a collage on the page. In the center, I'll glue the picture of us stuffing our faces with cotton candy.

Signed,
Summer, who says "Happy Birthday" to
the Aunt Alice I never really met

March 10

Dear Metti,

Tonight in Group, we talked about what the hardest thing is about living with a parent who has Evil Agent A. Lindsey explained how it's much harder living with someone in their mid-50s with Alzheimer's than an 88-year-old with Alzheimer's.

Jonathan answered first. The hardest thing for him is the decline in the quality of his mom's life. He remembers doing a lot of things with her. They would go hiking, canoeing, or biking, or they'd visit parks, and they both love to swim. Those activities are now in the background of their lives. Lindsey suggested starting up new but less physical activities, like bowling or going to the pool, not to swim laps but to relax. There's ping-pong, arcade games, or pool (as in the pool table kind of pool).

I shared with the group about the Tuesday Time that Mom and I try to have every Tuesday. I was a bit nervous that they would think it was babyish to spend time with your mom every Tuesday. Instead, I think some of them were jealous. I shared with them the activities we have done, anything from baking to playing Skee Ball to eating pizza while talking in a royal British accent.

Paige thought this was way cool and wanted to start something like it with her dad. Eric said he thought once a week would be too much time with his aunt Sarah. He would be open to twice a month. Jonathan didn't respond to it much, I guess because he feels he's too old. Chloe said that she shares a journal with her mom. They write back and forth over the course of the week, then start all over the next week. I almost spilled the beans and told them how I keep a journal named Metti. But I caught myself just in time.

Eric shared that the hardest thing for him is his aunt forgetting everything all the time. Well, no, not forgetting everything. She can remember the flavor of her first ice cream cone. But she can't remember where the extra rolls of toilet paper are in the bathroom. Eric said this drives him crazy! We all chimed in and told him to write things down for her, so she can read it as many times as she needs to help her remember.

Chloe said the hardest for her is her mom's depression. Her mom is on medicine, but she forgets to take it on a regular basis, so it doesn't work as it should. Chloe set an alarm on her mom's phone to remind her, but sometimes her mom forgets that the alarm just went off! Chloe can't stand seeing her mom looking so sad, like a puppy kicked in the stomach one too many times (her words, not mine). It's hard to cheer her up or get her out of bed to do anything so she'll feel better. Lindsey said if Chloe could motivate her mom, they could get into a swimming pool. There's something about water that regenerates and recharges one's body and soul.

I shared that the hardest thing about my mom's Alzheimer's is the roller coaster ride I feel I'm on from day to day. One minute we are all good, talking and sharing our ideas and our plans. Next thing I know, she's telling me about a baseball game she went to with her grandfather. I can laugh at the hallucinations; I can talk her through her steps in trying to find something she's misplaced. But the lack of normal, steady focus is what drives me crazy. It makes it so hard to talk to her. I miss having our deep conversations. I told them I write things down, draw pictures, and even do some coloring. Lindsey asked me if it helps, and I think it does.

Metti, this group is so good for me. Everyone is helpful in their own individual way. Of course, Lindsey is the most helpful, being the leader of the group. I am honestly thankful for each one of them. Thank you to Jonathan, Eric, Chloe, Paige, and JT for listening and for your support.

Signed,
Summer, who knows that we are all in this together

P.S. *Oh, and a BIG thank you to Lindsey!!!*

March 16

Dear Metti,

Chloe's mom is dead. Just like that. DEAD. She killed herself. This time, it wasn't my mom. But what about next time?

I feel so raw inside. So much crying. A cold wind has swept through, and it feels like parts of me blew away with it. I'm a daughter. I have a mom. A mom who is still alive. Chloe is a daughter. She had a mom. And now, her mom is dead.

This whole bad dream is going full nightmare. She killed herself. Just like that. She walked into her garage, making sure the doors were completely closed. Wearing her only fancy evening gown, she got in her car, sat in the driver's seat, turned on the engine, and sat willingly in her sealed tomb.

She left a letter saying how much she loved her family. She wrote about how proud she was of Chloe in everything she has done and will do. But how's a letter supposed to make Chloe feel better now?

Chloe's mom wanted the ultimate control in her life. She didn't want to die, losing her mind, her love, and her life to Alzheimer's. So that's that. She died on her own terms, at the hands of herself.

Signed,
Summer . . . gone numb

March 17

Dear Metti,

I don't feel much like writing. All I do is cry. Mom let me stay home today. She said that it could count as a death in the family.

I asked her, "What do I say when you die? Another death in the family?"

Mom shot me a look full of fear and determination mixed together, like swirling storm clouds. "Summer, having Alzheimer's is what it is. It can't be changed. And the only way we can fight it is to stick together and do our best. We can't hide from it. We can't run away from it. We can't leave it somewhere and pretend to lose it."

Then she looked straight into my eyes and made a promise that she will not take her own life. She said, "Summer, I hate to say this, but truth be told, Chloe's mom did the wrong thing." She made it very clear to me how it would be easier for Chloe to keep dealing with her mom's Alzheimer's than deal with her mom's suicide. In my mom's book, only cowards commit suicide. Chloe's mom was totally being selfish. She didn't give an ounce of thought to the mess she left behind. Abandoning a daughter who still needed her mother, Alzheimer's or not.

Here, I'm writing away again when I just told you that I don't feel much like writing. Metti, writing to you keeps me sane. And right now, I feel like I could go insane very, very, easily.

Signed,

Summer, who's on the brink of insanity

March 18

Dear Metti,

Chloe's mom's funeral is on the 21st. (By the way, her name was Mary.) My mom said I didn't have to go. She was afraid a raging storm of memories would rip through me again. The funeral of funerals that I will never forget for as long as I live is my dear friend's funeral. Like for real, it's going to be hard to go, if I go. I want to be there to support Chloe. I remember how important it was for people to be at Mettisha's funeral to support her family. It's going to be open casket. This I'm not used to. Mettisha's was closed casket. Mom says that open casket just shows the person at peace as if they are sleeping.

I told Mom I'd think about it. I really want to be there for Chloe. Going to the support group really does get you close to each other. I mean, we share so much about ourselves.

I don't think I've told you what we call our group. We call ourselves the "Alterheimers." So much of our lives are "altered" by living with someone with Alzheimer's. We wanted to keep it upbeat as much as possible.

I think some of the others in Group are going to go. Metti, there's so much to think about. I feel like my youthful world is being erased from my life. Forrest is moving home at the end of May to help me with Mom. See? Another life altered by Mom's Alzheimer's. Forrest isn't sure what to do after he graduates from the community college. He'll only have an associate's degree. His dream is to get a master's degree, maybe all the way to a doctorate. I feel bad about that, but so psyched my big brother will be home.

I'm going to school tomorrow, so off to bed. I wonder if I'll see Jason. I haven't said much of anything to him or even thought about him. How I wish I could turn back time. You know, turn back time before my mom's illness, before Jason's brother's arrest, before Jason and I broke up, even before my parents' divorce. Maybe if they were still married, all of this wouldn't be happening. Or, at least, Dad would be home to help take care of Mom so Forrest could finish his educational dreams. Oh, how I wish, I wish I could turn back time.

Signed,

Summer, who wants to build a time machine

March 19

Dear Metti,

I was such a slug today in school. Everybody around me was moving so quickly, while I sat there, watching them so slowly. I didn't raise my hand for a single thing all day long. I hardly talked to anyone. To top it off, my mom had a bad day. She couldn't believe there wasn't any dog food in the house. We haven't had a dog for years. When I was about seven years old, our dog, Callie, died, and we never got another pet.

My mom was not only freaking out that there wasn't any dog food. She was in a full-blown panic because there wasn't any dog, either! There was no way of reasoning with her. So, I let her live in her world for a while. Then, I calmly told her the reality of things. When she has moments like this, she tires herself out enough that usually, after we talk, she falls asleep. And so do I.

Signed,
Summer, who is feeling lonely.
Maybe I should get a dog.

March 20

Dear Metti,

My Alterheimer's meeting wasn't the same at all! Lindsay said that Chloe is now in a different group. She's in a group for teens who have lost a loved one. Her new group will help her work through mourning over her mom's suicide.

Hardly anyone talked tonight. Lindsey encouraged us to share how we were feeling. All was quiet.

Then, BANG! Eric stood up, kicked his chair over, and yelled, "CRAP! That's what we're feeling like: CRAP! And we aren't even the ones who are sick! What am I going to do when my aunt decides to kill herself? I have hardly anyone left. They're all dying!" He yanked up his chair and sat down hard. He hid his face from us as he started to cry with curse words under his breath. Within seconds, Jonathan was on one side of him, and Paige was on the other. They both wrapped their arms around him and tried to console him.

Lindsey was so calm. She gently told Eric that we need to fight one monster at a time. We have the control within ourselves to do that. His aunt Sarah is still very much alive. Her battle is going to be different than Chloe's mom's battle. Every Alzheimer's patient is unique. No one has the disease exactly in the same way. Some patients go downhill faster than others.

Lindsey talked about how she knows people who have the disease, and it has leveled out for years. For others, it goes much faster. Researchers are constantly working on finding medicines that help, or better yet, finding a cure. She couldn't stress enough how one guardian's suicide doesn't mean that all of our guardians are going to kill themselves. You live, love, and deal with what is in front of you—the here and now. Tomorrow's issues will be for another day—tomorrow.

Eric said that he didn't think he could go to Chloe's mom's funeral. Jonathan offered to give him a ride. Eric said that wasn't the problem. Then we all asked what the problem was. He didn't say anything. He just stared at the floor with his jaw bone clinched tightly. We all started to think it was because he was afraid to go.

Lindsey sensed it and didn't miss a beat. She told us that everyone deals with death differently. Some people don't face the person's death until years later, while others deal with it right afterwards. Then there are those who deal with it more in balance. No one way is better than the other. The key is that you feel and heal in your own time, at your own pace.

I'm pretty sure I'll go to the funeral. But I have no idea how it's going to affect me. It's a chance I'll just have to take for Chloe's sake.

Signed,
Summer, who wants to support her friend

March 21

Dear Metti,

Today is Chloe's mom's funeral. And my mom made me go to school. I totally did not feel like it! I told her that I was useless as a thinking, functioning human being. Mom said that the distraction of school would help me keep my mind off of things. She preached that if she can go to work, then I can go to school. I was so mad! She even drove me because she didn't trust me to get on the bus.

Well, I made it through the end of third period. Then I went to the nurse. I had a bad headache and my stomach was upset, so Mrs. Martin let me lay down, and I fell asleep. Our school nurse knows my mom because she volunteers at the library. I don't know if she knows about my mom having Alzheimer's. In fact, I don't know of anyone who knows. Like, how do you tell people? Something to ask the group about next meeting. Speaking of Group, I hope others make it to the funeral. I'll try to tell you more later. (I wrote this in study hall.)

March 21 (later)

Dear Metti,

Mom and I just got back from the funeral. My mom was right. Mary looked like she was going to wake up and talk to us any minute. But instead, she just lay there in a very cushioned casket, asleep forever.

There were a ton of people showing their support to Chloe and her father. Jonathan and Paige were there from Group. We sat near each other. I couldn't focus on the service or what the minister was saying. I just kept staring at Chloe, then at the casket, and back to Chloe. She sat so rigid. I'm sure she was crying. But it was hard to tell.

After the service, Chloe and her dad stood in a line, greeting people. My mom and I walked through. When I got to Chloe, I hugged her tightly. We both cried into each other's shoulders. I told her I'd text her. She said that would be great. But we both knew that it was going to be different from now on.

Metti, it was wrong for Chloe's mom to kill herself. No matter how her Alzheimer's affected her, Chloe needed her mom. Her real mom put her up for adoption, and now her adoptive mom is dead. NOT FAIR TO CHLOE! I'm so glad that my mom and I see it the same way. God takes you in His time—not too early and not too late. In His time.

Signed,

Summer, who's becoming very serious

March 25

Dear Metti,

I haven't written for a while. I just needed to take a break. I slept like all weekend. I feel sort of better. At least I have some energy. Today is Tuesday, and as you know, Mom and I are still sticking to our Tuesday Time. We both don't feel much like doing anything, but Mom says we need to do something to keep us going.

We went to this coffee house that opened about a month ago. It's called For the Love of Coffee. So I said to my mom, "If this place is all about the love of coffee, it would be a very good idea for me to get some coffee." She totally blew me away and said that I could order any coffee flavor, but it had to be decaf. Absolutely no problem here! I ordered the Mint Mocha Surprise. I can still taste it.

This was just what we needed. Sitting in a cozy atmosphere, sipping on soothing coffee while listening to soft guitar music. It relaxed us so much we even laughed. It's during times like these that I forget she has a disease. She acts her normal April Whitcomb self. It's during these times I just sit motionless, willing myself to soak it all in, so it'll be on reserve for when she isn't herself.

Signed,
Summer, "For the Love of Coffee"

March 26

Dear Metti,

I went into the freezer today to heat up leftover pizza. I saw something glittery on top of a bag of frozen peas. It was one of my mom's more expensive necklaces. I find things of hers all over the place. But this one takes the prize. At least she's hiding her valuables in a place that robbers wouldn't think of.

Signed,
Summer the treasure finder

March 27

Dear Metti,

Tonight I went to Alterheimer's. Things aren't going to be the same without Chloe in our group. It was Chloe who inspired "Evil Agent A," which kind of became the mascot to our Alterheimer's group. Being the youngest, she took on the role of being everyone's little sister. She didn't speak up all that much during group talks. But when she did, she had some wise stuff to say.

Lindsey told us that, despite any change in people around us, in our loved ones, or even within ourselves, there's one constant truth: We must live each day like it's our last day on Earth. She wasn't trying to be morbid. She just wanted us to see that to live is to love. And to love is to live. She's so right. (I think I've read that in a book somewhere.)

Signed,

Summer, who's getting wiser by the minute

March 29

Dear Metti,

Today was a rough day. Mom wasn't too off. It's just that I'm getting tired. It's getting harder keeping up with my schoolwork. I've told some teachers what's going on, but not in great detail. I don't want Children and Youth coming in and taking me away because Mom is having trouble taking care of me. Like, hello, I'm 13 years old! (Soon to be 14.) I'm pretty independent. I can do my own laundry and cook simple meals!

Metti, I feel like there's a black space consuming our lives. There's so much unknown all around us. But unknown doesn't have to mean bad, right? It can mean a chance to explore. Then the big question is: am I brave enough to do it? My mom is still my mom. We're in this battle together. I just hope I'm strong enough to fight for her. I know with all my heart she'd do the same for me.

Signed,
Summer, who wishes she was Joan of Arc

March 30

Dear Metti,

Well for the next twenty-thousand years of my life, I'll be helping my mom clean out our attic. For our Tuesday Time, she announced that we are going to start cleaning out our attic. And this is because. . . oh, yeah, Forrest is coming back home to live with us. That part I'm totally psyched about! According to Mom, we have to clean out the attic to make room for some of his old stuff to be stored for his newer stuff to be moved in. Why do I have to help? It's his stuff. According to my mother, it'll be fun doing it together, and she's willing to pay me. I'm in.

It wasn't too bad until the dust got to my allergies. We found all sorts of memory makers. There was a box full of ballet recital costumes of mine from when I was five years old. We found scout uniforms and sports uniforms. The big find for me was seeing Mom's wedding dress. I fell in love with it and swore I'd be wearing it as my own wedding dress. That's when my mom started to cry. (Yeah, there's been a lot of that lately.) But this time she said they were "happy tears."

We found some old stuff of my dad's that he didn't take with him. I thought for sure Mom was going to burn it, or at least throw it all away. Instead, she put it all in a box, pushing it into a corner of the attic.

As a reward for my hard work, we got some ice cream. And she paid me in cold, hard cash!

Signed,

Summer, who is sneezing again and again

P.S. *I'm putting a dust ball and tissue in mom's special book with a stick drawing of me blowing my nose!*

March 31

Dear Metti,

School went by fast today, and Group tonight went so slow. Usually, it's the other way around. For some reason, everyone in Group kept to themselves. There wasn't much sharing, and not even much answering Lindsey's questions to get conversation going. Before ending for the night, Lindsey gave us a homework assignment to hand in at our next meeting. She told us to write a letter to Chloe. Now that Chloe is in another support group, we need to have our own kind of closure. Some of us complained about doing it, because it meant there would be writing involved. But we all agreed to do this for Chloe. Group just isn't the same without her.

Signed,

Summer, who wants Chloe back

April 3

Dear Metti,

I can't believe I still get so excited about my birthday, like I used to when I was little. It's about two in the morning, and I can't sleep because today is my birthday. I know it's after midnight, so technically it's April third—my birthday. But no, it's not, because I wasn't born until 4:17 am. So technically, my mom would have two more hours of labor. Happy Birthday to me!

Signed,
Summer, who will never be
13 years old ever again!

April 3

Dear Metti,

Leave it to my mom. She came in my room at 4:17 am, blew a party horn in my ear to wake me up, and put a party hat on my head. She shuffled me down the stairs to the kitchen, where my birthday cake was all lit up in candle flames. I blew out my candles, making a wish to go back to bed. There we sat at the kitchen table, eating birthday cake as our very early breakfast. I went back to bed but couldn't sleep because now I'm on a sugar high. It's officially Happy Birthday to Me.

Signed,
Summer, who has been 14 years old
for 65 minutes of her life

April 5

Dear Metti,

Mom had a bad day today. I didn't know this, but things have been getting really hard for her at work. She struggles with remembering book titles, patrons' names, barcodes, and the simple process of checking books out. She came home in tears. She can deal with most of this, but what's heartbreaking for her is not being able to remember titles and authors of books. All her life, she breathed books. Now she's having a hard time breathing.

Signed,
Summer, who wants to help

April 7

Dear Metti,

   Alterheimer's was special tonight. We all wrote our letters to Chloe. We went around our circle to read our letters out loud if we wanted to. Some of the letters were funny, but some were serious.

   After sharing them, we all wondered what the use was if we couldn't share our feelings with Chloe. Then came the surprise! Chloe walked in the room, crying and smiling all at the same time. She had been waiting out in the hallway so she could surprise us. Well, we surprised her too. She thanked us for writing our letters. She wants to put them in a special kind of book so she can read and re-read them whenever she wants to. Particularly when times get rough.

   Then emotions went everywhere. We were hugging her, crying with her, laughing with her, and loving her. For the rest of our time, we drank soda and ate junk food. Lindsey played music and told us it was mandatory for everyone to dance. We were all good to go on that one! Dance we did!

Signed,
Summer, who showed her moves

April 9

Dear Metti,

My mom can't take the medicine she's been on. Her medical doctor called her today and told her that the side effects are affecting the color of her poop. Sounds gross, but when the person's poop becomes a weird color, then there's concern that something else is being affected in a bad way. I didn't ask her for details, because I don't want to know. All I want to know is what the new medicine is going to be. Mom said the doctors are working on it.

Signed,
Summer, who wishes with all her might
for someone to find a cure

April 14

Dear Metti,

Tonight during Group, I hope I didn't say something wrong that could get me in trouble. I shared with the group how I'm getting scared living with my mom. Ever since she had to go off her medicine because the doctor told her she had to, well, she's been getting mean. She yells at me lots more. She bangs things, rips things up, and throws perfectly good food away. She opens the refrigerator and takes food off the shelves, dumping it in the trash can. I can't reason with her. I can't get in her way. I'm too scared.

After Group, Lindsey talked to me alone. She told me I did the right thing by speaking up. My safety is top priority. She assured me that I wasn't in trouble, or my mom. However, the time has come for a visiting nurse to be at our house. Even when Forrest comes home (I'm counting the days), we still need a professional in the house to help us out.

This, of course, needs to be explained to my mom. The tricky part might be getting my mom to consent to it. I said a little prayer for my mom to do that. I'm seeing more of the Evil Agent A these days than I see of my mother.

Signed,
Summer, who wants to
do the right thing for her mom

April 16

Dear Metti,

When I came home today from school, Forrest was here. I was so happy to see him! He isn't home for good just yet. That won't be until May 14th. He came home to be sure I was okay. He plans on staying the weekend. He told me Lindsey called him and filled him in because a certain younger sister won't call him. He's right on that.

Monday, the visiting nurse starts. YES! Forrest talked with Mom, and she was okay with it. He presented it as a temporary situation until she gets on new medicine. The nurse's name is Alice. Alice Shoemaker. Alice is a nice name. I hope this works.

Signed,
Summer, who's hoping Alice
isn't from Wonderland.
(Again, the librarian's daughter emerges.)

April 19

Dear Metti,

Nurse Alice Shoemaker is WONDERFUL!!!!!! She's like Mrs. Claus. Not just because she's a bit chubby with graying hair. She's just so helpful. She talked with my mom for a while. Then she talked with me. But not about the Alzheimer's stuff. We talked about school and homework and my friends and who's my favorite teacher. We talked about normal stuff. She brought us baked goodies. She loves to bake. She made herself right at home without overdoing it. I think this is going to work out just fine.

Signed,
Summer, who has a good
feeling about this!!!!!

April 20

Dear Metti,

For today's Tuesday Time, I took Mom out mini golfing. And of all things, we tied. We both scored 56. We aren't sure if that's a good score or not. What we do know is a rematch is happening this summer. There was this one hole where I scored a hole in one. But it took Mom seven tries to get her ball in. At another hole, I took six shots to get my ball in the hole, while she got a hole in one. We just kept going back and forth with both of us winners in the end.

Signed,

Summer, who is going to secretly practice for the rematch

P.S. *I glued the score card in her special book.*

April 21

Dear Metti,

Alterheimer's group was rough tonight. Lindsey challenged us to think about our own definition of Alzheimer's. Up to this point, I didn't want to know much about it. I guess I thought that the more I knew, the more I would have to be scared of.

So, during our meeting, Lindsey told us a few facts about Evil Agent A. I didn't know Alzheimer's was the last name of the doctor who discovered the disease. Back in 1906, there was a doctor by the name of Alois Alzheimer. During this time, a woman died from what everybody thought was just "the crazies." This doctor thought differently, because when he studied her brain (after she was dead, of course), he found that mass around her brain was getting smaller, and the brain nerve cells were too. This shrinkage caused her to have memory loss, language problems, and unpredictable behavior. Which up until then, people labeled as having "the crazies."

"Alzheimer's can be a fight for anyone. Back in 1994, former President Reagan was diagnosed with having Alzheimer's." Lindsey likes to describe it more as a "fight" than a disease. She says if you think of it as a "fight," then you have a better chance of wanting to be the winner rather than a victim to the disease.

Jonathan shouted out that he would change his name and leave the country if he had a disease named after him. JT said that it's cool to have a disease named after you if you're the one who discovered it. He said that people would rather know what it is than not know what it is. He feels that there's power in knowledge. Paige was shocked that even rich, famous people like President Reagan got Alzheimer's.

Then I spoke up. "But the woman died from Alzheimer's."

Lindsey assured us that so much has been researched and improved since 1906. The breakthrough medicine Cognex has made great progress in Alzheimer's patients.

But I argued with her, almost yelling at her, about how my mom can't take that medicine anymore because of bad side effects. She told me doctors are finding new ways to deal with the same medicines. The FDA (the government people who test new drugs to be sure they're safe to take) have found that combinations of drugs help with the symptoms, making it possible for patients who have had bad side effects move forward in their treatment. Before I knew it, everyone was hugging me, while I just sat and cried.

Signed,
Summer, who is losing hope
and hopes Lindsey is right

April 22

Dear Metti,

I talked to Nurse Alice today. I told her all about what we talked about in Group last night. She has been working with Alzheimer's patients for eight years. And over those eight years, she has seen lots and lots of strange things. But the one thing she's seen that makes the Alzheimer's lose strength is hope. When people start losing their hope, their faith, their love, then the battle becomes a war. She told me not to lose sight of my hope, my faith, and my love. Battles are a lot easier to win than wars.

Signed,
Summer, who is ready to become a
five-star general against Alzheimer's!

April 25

Dear Metti,

My mom is still my mom. Today, she informed me that
lemons are deadly. So, she threw out all the lemons. I barely
had time to save the lemonade from a similar fate. I'm hiding it
in plain sight. I put a pineapple juice label over the lemonade
label. The juices are about the same color. Anyway, it worked
like a charm.

Signed,

Summer, who can come up with
some pretty good saves

P.S. *I have to remember to tell Alice*
not to make us a lemon meringue pie.

April 27

Dear Metti,

Thank goodness for Nurse Alice. Mom didn't go to work today, so when I got home, there was a note on the kitchen table letting me know that Mom and Alice had gone out. There wasn't a lot of detail. She wrote that Mom needed to be somewhere else for a little while.

"A little while" turned out to be 8:20 at night. Nurse Alice had taken Mom to the ER. Mom came home with stitches above her eye and her arm in a sling. Obviously, I got really upset. Nurse Alice took care of Mom by putting her to bed. She asked me if I'd had dinner. I told her I'd made myself a big snack. Nurse Alice went to a fast food restaurant to buy herself some dinner and came back with some for me too. As we crunched on french fries, she told me the whole story.

Mom went into a fit about the dryer being a fallout shelter. Mom thought there was a war going on. So, she ran downstairs opened up the dryer and tried to get herself inside of it for protection. Nurse Alice couldn't reason with her. When Alice tried to pull her out, Mom got really upset and started taking swings at Alice. Alice had to restrain my mom, which they are trained to do when things get thick. But there was a struggle, and Mom hit her head on the dryer door and sprained her arm as she was trying to get away from Nurse Alice.

Alice said she was sorry for my mom getting hurt. I leaned over and hugged her. I didn't want to let go. I didn't want her to leave.

Signed,
Summer, who can't wait for this
bad, bad dream to be over

261

April 28

Dear Metti,

Tonight at Alterheimer's group, if we wanted to, we could share our definitions of what Alzheimer's is. Not many of us had done the homework. In fact, it was just me and Jonathan. Jonathan went first. His definition was, "Alzheimer's is a leech-type creature that sucks out brain cells, blood cells, organ cells, eyeball cells, any kind of cell. Alzheimer's is a creature yet to be tamed before it kills us all."

After Jonathan, I shared my definition. I read it from a piece of loose-leaf paper, so I'll just copy it out here.

"I, Summer Ray Whitcomb, declare the following as the definition of my mother's Alzheimer's disease:

"A soldier skilled in silent warfare has invaded my mother's body. He has marched his way up the spiral staircase, leading him to the top of her head. This is where he has set up camp. Slowly and faithfully, he has built a prison around her brain. Trapped behind thick steel bars, secured by keyless locks, all mental pathways are blocked, with little to no hope for escape. Darkness and hallucinations are her constant cellmates. There are no more sparks to her creativity, imagination, or intellect. Her free spirit has been flogged. Alzheimer's is an enemy of mine. And it is destroying my world!"

After I read this, everyone was quiet, like in a movie theatre during the climax scene. All the silence ended when they started clapping. Lindsey said that what I'd written was deep in meaning and rich in words. She thought that someone years older than me should have written what I wrote. It made me feel good that they valued my writing. In fact, they liked my writing. But I was sad at the same time, because what I wrote was very depressing. And very real, even if it was a metaphor.

Signed,
Summer, who took a chance
in sharing and didn't throw up

May 4

Dear Metti,

My mom was in charge of our Tuesday Time this week. You wouldn't believe what she did. Remember when I said that I'd been helping her clean out our attic for the next twenty-thousand years to make room for Forrest's stuff? Well, that was all a lie.

Mom took me up to the attic, and there on the far left side was this area, set up all cozy-like. Let me describe it to you. Enclosing the area are these huge, hanging scarves with paisley patterns on them. (My mom likes paisley patterns.) Inside the curtained area, there is a forest green shag rug—my mom's favorite color. Leaning up against the beamed walls of the attic are these oversized, sunset-colored pillows. Colors of soft pink, orange, and twilight blue. My mom loves looking at the sky, especially at sunset. There are two bookcases. One bookcase is full of books of all kinds. There are big photo albums, baby board books, favorite picture books, old worn out books, and books written by my mom's favorite authors—mostly Gary Paulsen. On the other bookcase, there are family pictures all in silver frames. My mom loves silver. She never would consider herself a woman of gold. There are pictures of her with us, pictures of her by herself, and even a few pictures of her and my dad.

When Mom saw me staring at the pictures, she told me that this is the Tuesday Time Travel Room. If and when things get bad with my mom, I'm supposed to come up here and be with the April Whitcomb she used to be. To be with the April Whitcomb who's a free spirit, a lover of words, an advocate of books, always a librarian at heart; a mother with no regrets; a woman who dreams of having breakfast with Gary Paulsen, her all-time favorite author; and a woman who doesn't want to be forgotten as who she was and who she is. My mom made a haven for Forrest and me to find shelter when the Alzheimer's storm spins our lives out of control. I hugged her and cried into her shoulder, not tears of sadness, but tears of relief.

I knew this was the right time to give her the book I've been making this past year. So, I ran downstairs and grabbed it. I ran back up to the attic, hoping Evil Agent A would take the night off. I wanted my mom to mentally stay with me.

I handed her the book. Before even opening it up or knowing what it was all about, she started crying happy tears! I showed her all the pages I'd composed from gathering the memory items. We giggled over the "royal talking" dinner. We challenged each other to rematches in bowling and Skee Ball and mini golf. I blushed when we came to the page about going to Jason's soccer game. (That feels like a hundred years ago!) We got hungry looking at the pictures of our baked apple pie, gingerbread houses, and ice cream outings. She loved my drawings and my little quirky sayings. She loved everything I put into it and everything it meant to me for her.

Mom kissed the cover and placed it on the top shelf of the bookcase. We sat down on the super soft shag rug and fell into the super soft pillows. We lay there, holding the moment as mother and daughter, as it should be, without memory loss, unpredictable behavior, language problems, or misplaced things.

Metti, when I become a mother, I will have Tuesday Time with my child. I will value it as I value it now. My mother is always there for me. Sometimes it's only half of her, but she still is there.

Signed,
Summer, who just might even give her child a diary on their 13th birthday!

About the Author

For more than twenty years, Amy has been learning from children. Her years of work experience range from learning centers to summer camps to elementary schools. For the past eleven years, Amy has been on an adventure—not on a "magic school bus," but on a bookmobile serving as driver and mobile librarian. She considers it a privilege to be in a position to touch the minds of the next generation through the power of words. Amy has been writing since she was ten years old. She has a degree in English writing and literature, and two diplomas from the Institute of Children's Literature. When Amy isn't reading or writing, she enjoys swimming and spending time with her family at home in Elizabethtown, PA. However, Amy's home away from home is the children's section of any library or bookstore. Visit Amy online at www.amyewhitman.com.